Praise for the Bluford Series:

"Once I started reading, I couldn't sleep. My hands were sweating and my heart was pumping. I thought something was wrong with me. These books are *that* exciting."
— *Kareem S.*

"I love the Bluford Series because I can relate to the stories and the characters. They are just like real life. Ever since I read the first one, I've been hooked."
— *Jolene P.*

"On a scale of 1–10, the scale breaks if I rate the Bluford Series. They are *that* good!"
— *Cornell C.*

"The last thing I wanted to do was read a Bluford book or any book. But after a few pages, I couldn't put the book down. I felt like I was a witness in the story, like I was inside it."
— *Ray F.*

"I found it very easy to lose myself in these books. They kept my interest from beginning to end and were always realistic. The characters are vivid, and the endings left me in eager anticipation of the next book."
— *Keziah J.*

"Man! These books are amazing!"
— *Dominique J.*

"Usually I don't like to read, but I couldn't put the Bluford books down. They kept me interested from beginning to end."
—*Jesus B.*

"My school is just like Bluford High. The characters are just like people I know. These books are real!"
—*Jessica K.*

"I thought the Bluford Series was going to be boring, but once I started, I couldn't stop reading. I had to keep going just to see what would happen next. I have to admit I enjoyed myself. Now I'm done, and I can't wait for more books."
—*Jamal C.*

"All the Bluford books are great. There wasn't one that I didn't like, and I read them all—twice!"
—*Sequoyah D.*

"I've been reading these books for the last three days and can't get them out of my mind. They are *that* good!"
—*Stephen B.*

"Each Bluford book gives you a story that could happen to anyone. The details make you feel like you are inside the books. The storylines are amazing and realistic. I loved them all."
—*Elpiclio B.*

"All my friends and I agree. The Bluford Series is bangin'!"
—*Margarita R.*

The Fallen

Paul Langan

Series Editor: Paul Langan

TOWNSEND PRESS
www.townsendpress.com

Books in the Bluford Series

Copyright © 2007 by Townsend Press, Inc.
Printed in the United States of America

9 8

Cover illustration © 2007 by Gerald Purnell

ISBN-13: 978-1-59194-066-1
ISBN-10: 1-59194-066-4

Library of Congress Control Number:
2006922148

Chapter 1

"Martin, do you have anything to say for yourself?" Mr. Gates says to me. I can hear anger in his voice.

He's the superintendent of Bluford High School—a large silver-haired man in his late 60s. His lips are pencil-thin, and there are bags under his eyes. Bags from listening to stories like mine.

I know he's going to throw me out of Bluford. I can't blame him. All he knows about me is what he's read in the thick folder on his desk.

I can see the pink suspension notices from my seat. He flips through them like he's leafing through an old phone book. I know the words he's reading. I remember the last letter the school district sent to my mother.

MARTIN LUNA has on multiple occasions displayed severe behavioral problems in school and on school grounds. He has repeatedly engaged in threatening and hostile confrontations with other students, and he has violated school attendance policies numerous times. Furthermore, given his most recent outburst, it is the opinion of this district that he poses a threat to students and faculty. As a result, the district recommends that MARTIN LUNA be expelled from Bluford High School.

My mother cried when she got the letter. I found it laying on our kitchen counter stained with teardrops that made the ink bleed. I crumpled it up right then, but it didn't matter. The damage was done.

Today's my hearing—my last chance.

"Well?" he says. He's looking at me now. He doesn't even blink.

The auditorium is quiet except for someone coughing as I stand to answer him. I hear my mother sniffle behind me. *I'm so sorry for everything, Ma,* I want to say. I feel guilt clawing at my

2

chest like invisible hands.

"Please don't do this," my mother yells out. "He's a good boy. *Please!*" I turn to see her standing at her seat, holding her hands as if she's praying to him. Her nose is running and her voice is trembling. It reminds me of how she was three months ago, the day my little brother died. I close my eyes to push the memories back, but it doesn't work.

"Ms. Luna," Mr. Gates cuts in. "I understand this is difficult for you, but we've already heard what you had to say. Now *please* let your son speak."

My mother sits down, crosses herself, and quietly wipes her eyes. She's never backed down from anything, but this time I know she expects the worst. So do I.

Mr. Gates turns back to me. He closes my folder, drops his pen, and rubs his forehead like he's got a bad headache. I am in trouble. No question about it.

"Mr. Luna, in just two weeks at Bluford High School, you have been in several serious fights. You have cut school, skipped classes, and last Friday in the middle of yet another fight, you struck a teacher. This behavior is unacceptable. Unless there are some extenuating circumstances, I'm afraid we have no choice but to expel you. Now, this hearing is your opportunity to tell your side of the story. Martin, what do you have to say for yourself?"

I look up at him because some of his words escape me. *Extenuating circumstances*? I don't know what they are. But I do know there are reasons why I shoved old Mr. Dooling into a wall, why me and Steve Morris keep fighting, why my anger sometimes explodes like a gunshot.

I never meant for any of it to happen. I know I screwed up, especially when I pushed the teacher. But everything else I did was the best I could do, was the only choice I really had.

There's no way Mr. Gates will ever understand this. His eyes tell me what he thinks—expelling me is the right thing to do. There's no changing his mind. I can see that.

Still, like Vicky said, I gotta try. I take a deep breath and begin telling him the truth, how it started days ago when I stumbled into Bluford a bloody mess . . .

"Oh my God, Martin," Vicky said as she looked at the cut over my eye. Her mouth was wide open, and her hands covered her cheeks. "Who did this to you? Was it Steve?"

I shook my head no. I wished she didn't have to see me this way. I could taste blood in my mouth and knew some was on my face. She deserved to know what happened, but I had no time to explain. Frankie and the rest of my crew were on the road, and someone was about to get hurt. I had to do something. Now.

"I'm fine, Vicky. I'll catch up with you later," I said, but my voice cracked into a nasty whisper. I was dizzy. Too many punches to my head.

"Quick, Martin, inside right now," barked Ms. Spencer, our principal. She led me past Vicky straight to the front office. "The rest of you get back to class. There is nothing to see here."

It was almost time for first lunch period, and a small crowd of students had gathered at the front of the school to see my entrance. They looked at me as if I had just shot someone. *What are you starin' at?* I felt like saying, but I had more important things to worry about.

"Ms. Spencer, I need to speak with someone I know. He's a cop. His name is Nelson Ramirez. I need to speak with him. *Now*," I said. She studied my face carefully, not sure whether to trust me.

I couldn't blame her. Where I come from, you don't talk to cops, and you don't expect them to solve problems. I learned that when Huero, my little brother, was killed. For months, my mother and I waited for the police to do something. All we got from them was an apology and some excuses about workload and too many cases.

But Ramirez was different. He was Chicano like us, a friend of my mom's who grew up in the barrio. He held my mom at my brother's funeral and understood that the day Huero died, part of me died too. Where else could I turn?

"I already called the police, Martin." Ms. Spencer said as I collapsed into the squeaky chair in her office. "I called your mother, too. She's on her way," she added.

My headache was getting worse. The last thing I wanted was my mom to see me this way. But I didn't have time to worry about it.

"Call Ramirez," I repeated, rubbing my swollen jaw. "Here's his phone number. Tell him Martin Luna is looking for him." I handed her the crumpled piece of paper he'd given me over the summer.

"Why him?" Ms. Spencer asked, studying the scrap like it was a fake ID card or something. "If you did something wrong, now is the time to tell me so you won't get in any worse trouble."

I wanted to curse her out right there. Behind her wire-rimmed glasses, she couldn't see nothin'. I wasn't afraid of any punishment she could give me. A suspension? A letter? That ain't nothin' compared to watching your brother die in your arms, seeing his blood drip onto your shoes, feeling his skin turn cool in your hands. And now more blood was about to spill.

"There ain't no worse trouble!" I growled, tired of talking to her. I jumped up and reached for her office phone. But my legs were weak, and the room suddenly felt like waves were rolling through the floor. I leaned against the wall to stop from falling.

"*Martin!*" Ms. Spencer yelled, grabbing me and easing me back into the chair. Her eyes were wide with worry.

"*Please*, Ms. Spencer," I said, pointing to the phone.

"Okay, okay. I'm calling him right

now. Just sit down and don't move," she said, nervously dialing the numbers. "But if there is something I can do to protect you and the other students in this school, you need to let me know."

Protect me? Too late for that, I wanted to say. The room was spinning. I grabbed the chair to steady myself. "Just call him."

I knew it would come down to this. I knew it the second I agreed to meet my homeboys in the parking lot outside Bluford. Our crew—Frankie, Chago, Junie, and Jesus—were about to do something we had talked about since Huero died. We were going to get revenge.

After months of searching, we found out who shot my brother—a punk named Hector Maldenado. We'd talked about what we'd do all summer. For a while, I dreamed about it night and day. It was the only thing that pushed the hurt away. The only reason I had to get up in the morning.

Don't get me wrong, I ain't a gang-banger. I've stolen a few things and gotten into some fights, but I never did something serious like this before. But everything changed when Huero died. I snapped like an old rubber band.

Frankie Pacheco knew this. He was the oldest and toughest in our crew. He got us guns and showed us what we needed to know. And for a while I was ready to let it all go down like that.

Pop! Pop! Pop!

Just three shots. A blast of sour gun smoke. The screeching of tires as Frankie's old LeMans pulled away. The same sounds I heard the afternoon Huero died. That would be the end of it.

But I couldn't do it.

In my head, I kept seeing my brother's face, Vicky's eyes, my mom's tears. And I kept hearing something my English teacher, Mr. Mitchell, said. *You could have a bright future ahead of you. Don't throw it away.*

Call me soft. I don't care. You're not the one who sits at your brother's grave, listens to your mother crying in the dark, and knows what it's like to lose someone. If you were, you'd understand why I couldn't be like the coward who drove down our street and stole my brother's life with a gunshot.

"Yes, this message is for Officer Ramirez," Ms. Spencer said. "This is the principal at Bluford High School. I have

Martin Luna here in my office. He seems to have been involved in an altercation and wishes to speak with you. He says it's important."

I put my head in my hands. A message! Where was he? It was the one time I needed to reach him, and he wasn't there.

Call me anytime, he had said when he gave me the number. Yeah, right.

I felt Ms. Spencer watching me. I knew she was wishing I never transferred into her school. But if I'd stayed at Zamora High, I'd be in jail or dead already.

That's why my mom moved out of our old neighborhood, making me start my sophomore year at Bluford High. I was so angry when she told me, I almost punched her. Can you believe that? I hate when I get that way, but Huero's death did that to me.

The move added 45 minutes to her bus ride to Wal-Mart where she worked as a cashier with Nilsa, Frankie's older sister. But she did it—to *save* me. It didn't work.

"Where is he?" a man yelled into the office, shattering my thoughts. "Where's Martin?"

I looked up to see Mr. Mitchell. The

throbbing in my skull was worsening by the minute, and the room was fuzzy, like an old TV that isn't tuned in right.

"What happened?" he asked, shaking his head. The other day, he gave me an "A" for an essay I wrote about Huero. I wondered what he'd say if he knew another kid was about to die because I was too scared to talk.

I stared at him, my heart pounding. My hands sweating. The room seemed to spin. Overhead, the bell sounded, announcing the beginning of first lunch period. Time was running out like blood from a cut.

"Martin, what is it?"

I knew it would take Frankie at least a half hour to get to Hector's house. It hadn't been that long since we fought. If I acted now, there still was a chance I could do something. But I wasn't ready to rat out my boys. I ain't a snitch.

Up until a month ago, Frankie and I were like brothers. *Family*, he called me and the rest of our crew. I even took a beating to earn that word. That's how we did things.

But then Frankie admitted that the bullet that killed my brother was probably aimed at him. I don't know why I

11

never thought of it before, but it made sense. Frankie was the one with the knife wound, the homie most feared on our block, the tattoo-covered 19-year-old who had enemies everywhere. Of course the bullet was meant for him, not an eight-year-old boy. Not Huero.

The news changed me. It was like I'd been asleep and suddenly woke up. Questions kept popping in my head in the middle of the night, cutting our friendship like a knife. Making me secretly hate him. Why did Huero have to pay for what Frankie did? And why was Frankie free to cruise the 'hood while my brother's lying in the ground?

Frankie wasn't stupid. He knew I was changing. That's why he wanted me to do the shooting this morning. It would make me as guilty as him, and it would mean he'd always have something on me in case I gave him trouble. I'm sure he planned it this way. But he didn't plan on me backing out.

"I'm not doin' it, Frankie. I'm serious," I announced while we were all sitting in his LeMans ready to get Hector. The car got as quiet as a grave.

You should have seen Frankie's face. If it were a gun, I'd be dead right now. I jumped out before anyone could stop me.

Chago, my best friend from back in the day, tried to change my mind. He was worried about what Frankie would do next.

"C'mon, Martin. We're family, man. Brothers," Chago said. "Let's go."

The word stung me. *Family*. It was like a slap in my face. Look what the word did to me—it cost me my brother and was about to turn me into a criminal. That ain't what family is supposed to be. Anyone who says so needs to get their head examined.

"My brother was Huero, Chago," I said. "And he's dead because of something Frankie did. You know it's true. What we are about to do, it ain't family, Chago. It's crazy."

Frankie lost it. His jaw tightened up, and he got this cold look I saw once before when he jumped a kid for talking to his girlfriend. The guy was already on the ground when Frankie's foot smashed into his face with a heavy wet thud. I can still hear the sound. The guy moaned and threw up, and Frankie backed away, acting like he was trying to protect his new steel-tipped boots from the mess. Like they were more important than another person.

Frankie was ready to do worse to me when he stepped out of his car. Don't get me wrong. I can handle myself in a fight. But I'm no match for Frankie. His fists pounded into my face and side, knocking me to my knees. That's when he pulled out his gun.

"You can't leave your family, Martin," he said. His nine millimeter was pointed at my face. It was the first time I looked into the barrel of a gun.

All I could think about was the bloody mess I'd be when my mother found me, how she'd cry at my funeral with no sons at her side.

"I can't go no further. Do what you gotta do," I said. I whispered a prayer just in case.

Frankie blinked.

Maybe it was the guilt he had for Huero's death. Maybe it was that he didn't want to shoot me in daylight where a crowd of people could witness it. Or maybe it was because he was shocked that I was willing to die to prove I ain't a killer. I don't know what it was, but Frankie let me go.

"This ain't done," he growled and

jumped back into his car.

I believe him.

The clock over Ms. Spencer's desk said 10:38. Frankie and the boys had been on the road for 20 minutes already. There were at least two guns in the car, and the only one who knew their plan was me. I was wasting time.

"C'mon, Martin. It's like I said before. You have a choice. You can end this right now," Mr. Mitchell said, staring at me like I was a puzzle. "We're listening."

I could feel myself zoning out, like there was a fog settling over my brain. All last night, I replayed how this day would go down. When I grabbed my bandana and left to meet Frankie, I knew I had to walk away, that Frankie was gonna come at me like never before. But I figured if I could just escape and get to Bluford, it would all be over.

I was wrong.

Looking at Ms. Spencer's tight jaw and Mr. Mitchell's wide eyes, I knew it was just beginning.

Chapter 2

"He's in the principal's office, Ms. Luna. He's been hit in the head, and he's a little out of it. We have an ambulance coming to take him to the hospital," I heard Ms. Bader, the school secretary, say in the distance.

Instantly, the pounding in my head got worse.

I closed my eyes and listened as the familiar jingle of my mom's keys grew louder. Then I heard another sound. My mom gasping.

"Oh, Jesus, no!" she cried, darting across the office to me.

"I'm okay, Ma. It looks worse than it is," I said, shocked at who followed her into the office. It was Ramirez! Like always, my mom must have called him the second she knew something was wrong with me. No wonder he hadn't answered his phone.

"Who did this? *Who did this?!*" my mother yelled, brushing my hair and then hugging me. Her eyes were wet and bloodshot. I didn't want to see them. I pushed her away.

"Ma, I need to talk to Officer Ramirez now. It's important. Can you all leave us for a minute?"

Mr. Mitchell and Ms. Spencer stared at each other. My mom started shaking her head, the way she always does before she says no. I looked at Officer Ramirez. I needed him to listen to me.

"Please, Imelda. It will just be a minute," he said.

Mr. Mitchell almost looked hurt for a second, but he walked out of the office without a word. So did Ms. Spencer. Officer Ramirez closed the door behind them.

"What happened, Martin?"

I closed my eyes and took a deep breath. I was about to do something I never did before—talk to a cop. For a second I couldn't speak, like invisible hands were holding my mouth shut.

Snitch! I could hear a voice in my head insulting me. *Martin Luna's a snitch!*

That's one thing you don't do in the barrio, something I never did no matter how many times I got in trouble. But I kept thinking of Huero and what was about to happen in his name. I couldn't let it happen.

"I know who shot my brother," I said, careful to keep my friends' names hidden. "His name is Hector Maldenado, and he lives at 2187 Tanner Street. You need to throw his butt in jail before something really bad happens to him."

"Bad?" Ramirez said, studying my face. I knew he understood me. "How soon?"

"Like right now," I said, glancing up at the clock. "Get someone over there now, or it's gonna be too late."

"How do you know this?"

I shrugged my shoulder.

"Is Frankie Pacheco behind this?"

"I didn't say that." I knew I didn't have to. He was smart enough to figure that much out himself.

"Martin, if something happens to Hector, you and Frankie—"

"I didn't do nothin'!" I said before he could go any further. "And nothin's gonna happen if you leave right now. Go!"

My head felt like it was breaking apart. If you told me a month ago that I'd send out the police against my friends, I would have been all up in your face. Now look at me.

I just kept picturing Frankie and the boys rolling up on Hector only to have a dozen cop cars surround them. Either the cops would arrive early and catch Frankie with guns in his car, or they'd arrive too late and Hector would be shot.

Either way it played out, it was going to be bad. And I was at the center of it.

Martin Luna's a rat. That voice in my head wouldn't shut up.

Officer Ramirez bolted out of Ms. Spencer's office like someone whose house was burning down. Within seconds, Ms. Spencer, Mr. Mitchell, and my mother were back.

"What's happening, *mijo*? What did you tell him?" my mother asked, staring at me, her face pale like she was coming down with the flu or something. I felt sick too. Nauseous.

"Don't worry about it, Ma," I said, rubbing my forehead where Frankie clocked me. I could feel the lump there. And the blood in my hair. The pain.

My mother looked at my hands and

turned to Ms. Spencer. "Where's the doctor? How come you're all standing around? His head's bleeding!"

"The ambulance should be here any second, Ms. Luna." Ms. Spencer rubbed her own temples. She looked like she hadn't slept in days.

"Frankie did this to you, didn't he?" My mother gave me that look moms do when they think you're hiding something.

"It ain't like that, Ma," I said, my voice breaking. The less she knew, the better.

"The ambulance is out front," Ms. Bader called out.

"C'mon, *mijo*. Let's go. I'm going to ride with you."

I tried to stand up, but my balance was gone. The room spun like the inside of a washing machine. Even the fluorescent lights overhead became dim and hazy.

A paramedic got in my face and said something, but his words were slow and made no sense.

In the chair across the office, I noticed something strange.

A small boy, younger than any freshman. He was wearing a backwards Los

Angeles Angels baseball cap, and he was looking at me and smiling.

It was my little brother.

I'm so sorry for all this, Huero, I tried to say, but my words came out all mumbled.

"What did he just say?" the medic asked.

Tears filled my eyes. They burned as they snaked down my swollen face. I tried to reach out to Huero. To touch him again. But my arms were suddenly like dead weights and the world was fading around me.

I blinked and he was gone.

Then blackness . . .

I don't know how long I was out, but when I woke up, I was in a hospital bed wearing a papery gown. I felt naked and cold in that thing, but what woke me up even faster was the person at the foot of my bed.

It was Officer Ramirez.

"What happened?" I asked, sitting upright. I noticed my mother's jacket draped across a chair at the foot of the bed. My clothes were there too.

"You're in the hospital, Martin. Whoever hit you gave you a concussion.

You got a few stitches too, but you're all right. The doctors wanted to observe you for a while before they send you home. Now that you're awake, they'll probably get you outta here soon. Your mother's been here all day. She just went down to get a cup of coffee."

"But what happened with Hector? Did you get there on time?"

"Nothing happened, Martin," he said, crossing his arms on his chest. "We had people on Tanner Street, and I even had someone check out Frankie Pacheco's house . . . just in case," he said, eyeing me. I didn't blink. "He was working on his car when we found him. He kept at it all day."

My heart was pounding so loud I thought he could have heard it if he listened. *Nothing happened.* That meant I stopped them. Frankie changed his plans because of me. But what else did it mean? Was Frankie just giving up? And what about Hector? Was he in jail already? The questions flooded my head faster than I could speak.

"Listen, Martin. I want to applaud you for contacting me. Every day bad things happen in the city that could be prevented if someone were brave enough to take a stand. People complain all the time, but few are willing to step up and do something about it."

I ignored him. I wanted answers, not a pep talk.

"What about Hector? You got him, right?"

"Now listen, Martin," he said. I could tell by the way his voice hung in the air that he was going to say something I didn't want to hear. "We don't have any real proof that Hector did anything. He has no record, and he seems to spend his time with his family. Are you positive he shot Huero?"

I blinked. I couldn't believe my ears. Not again. Not another day with Huero's killer walking free.

"I know for a fact he did it," I blurted out.

"What proof do you have?"

I could feel my temper building. The truth was I hadn't seen anything that day except a white car with tinted windows. The only reason I knew Hector was involved was because Chago and Frankie told me. I knew they wouldn't lie, not about this, but I couldn't say that without bringing them into it. That would just make things worse.

"I just know he did it," I said.

"Well unless you can prove it, or you can get someone who knows to talk to us, we can't do anything except investigate. We can't just go arresting people on rumors, Martin."

His words were a slap in my face. After months of waiting, I couldn't listen to more excuses. For a second, I saw red. Blood red.

"*You see!* This is why people don't come to you. 'Cause when they do, no one believes them and nothin' gets done. I don't know why I even bothered with you. You're no different than the rest of them."

"C'mon, Martin. No one wants to solve your brother's murder more than me—"

"*I* do!" I screamed. "You think I took this beating for nothin'? It coulda all been different, *Officer*," I said, twisting the word into an insult. "If I'da known this is how it would end up, I wouldn'ta said nothin' to you." It was like a dam burst in my head, and my anger was just spilling out. I kept thinking about Huero. I saw him in my mind lying on the ground again, his life pouring through my fingers and dripping onto the concrete like red rain.

"You know *we* got ways of handing this without the police," I added, unable to stop myself. I knew my words sounded like a threat, but I didn't care.

"Now be careful, Martin. You did the right thing today. You had enough guts and sense to try to solve this the right way. Now stick with it. I don't want to find you on the street in a pool of blood, and I don't want you to waste your life in jail. You're a good kid, and your mom would do anything for you. You've got more going for you than a lotta kids out there. Stay at Bluford. Get your education, and do something with yourself. You hear me?" He put his hand on my shoulder like we were friends or something.

"Yeah, I hear you," I mumbled, shrugging off his hand. Who was he to tell me what I should be doing when he let a killer go free? "I hear you sayin' you're not gonna do nothin' about what happened to Huero."

He looked like I had just slapped him in the face. Part of me wanted to hit him too.

"Look, there's no point talking to you right now," Officer Ramirez said, taking a deep breath and turning away from me. "I'm going to keep my eyes and ears open, and we'll be watching Hector. We're not giving up on Huero."

"Whatever," I hissed, cursing under my breath. It was like old times, when anger was the only thing I felt.

"And listen, Martin," he added as he reached the doorway. "No matter what you do, stay away from Frankie. He looked like he expected us to be watching him today. He might even think you were the reason we were interested in him. I'm saying this to warn you. Stay away from him, and if he starts bothering you in any way, call me. You got it?"

"Yeah, I'll call you," I said, knowing I would never do it, not after this.

He sighed and walked out. I grabbed my clothes and changed out of the hospital gown. Not only was my little brother's killer still out there. Now Frankie, the guy who used to be like a big brother, might be coming after me. And the only person in his way was Officer Ramirez.

Please! He was useless. A bull's-eye painted on my chest would protect me better than him.

"*Mijo!* Thank God you're awake. You've been asleep for hours," my mother said, rushing in from the hallway to give me a hug. "Did you see Nelson?"

"Yeah. He just left," I said.

"I'm so proud of you for talking to him. He's been so good to us. I hope you thanked him for what he did."

Thanked him? *For what?* I wanted to say. Getting Frankie after me and letting Huero's killer go free? I didn't feel like fighting with her in the middle of the hospital. My head still hurt, and I was tired.

"Whatever, Ma," I said.

She sighed and put her hands on my face, forcing me to look at her.

"You scared me," she said. "If Nelson wasn't with us this morning, I would have lost it. He told me you did a brave thing and that I should be proud of you. Now I don't know what happened, and since you won't talk to me about it, I'm just going to say this once. I don't want you hanging out with any of your old friends. They're no good, Martin. I don't want you going back there anymore, not unless you're with me."

"*What?*" I yelled, feeling my old temper coming back. "That ain't right. What are you punishing me for?"

"I'm not punishing you, Martin. I'm

protecting you. I lost one son, and I'm not gonna lose another one. End of story."

"You don't know what you're talking about. Neither does Ramirez," I yelled. My world was crashing down, and everyone I knew was trying to make it worse.

"You can yell all you want, but you're not going to see them anymore," she said.

"Yeah, we'll see about that," I mumbled just loud enough for her to hear.

She glared at me, and I just looked away. I knew she was serious, but so was I. Huero was buried in our old neighborhood, and if I wanted to visit him, there was no way I was going to ask for permission. Not from her or anyone.

I was glad when the doctor came in and cut off our conversation. He checked my head and shined a light in my eyes.

"I'm gonna send you home tonight," he said. "But for the next two weeks, be gentle with your head. That means no gym class, no sports, and *please*, no fighting. Another shot to the head could cause permanent brain damage."

He spoke as if I had a choice about where Frankie hit me. My mother sighed at his last words, but I ignored her.

"Whatever you say, Doc," I replied.

It was getting dark when we finally left the hospital. My mother and I didn't speak to each other at all on the bus ride back. What was I going to say? All I wanted to do was yell.

When we stepped off the bus, I walked ahead of her to our apartment. As I neared our front step, I spotted something dark covering our doorknob, something that made my stomach drop and my heart race.

My black bandana.

I grabbed it before my mom noticed it. But I knew who had put it there. The same person who knocked it off my head earlier that day. The same one who wanted me to know I was in trouble.

Frankie.

Chapter 3

That night I didn't sleep.

I kept listening to the creaks and groans of our apartment, wondering if someone was watching us.

It's funny how many sounds the night makes, especially when you're nervous. At one point, I swear I heard someone walking in our kitchen. I even grabbed Huero's old baseball bat in case I needed to hit something.

Just some pipes in the wall making noise. I checked all the closets and then glanced out our living room window to make sure Frankie's LeMans wasn't out there. Nothing.

Somewhere far away, sirens screamed, and a memory of Huero's ambulance ride to the hospital flashed in my mind. My mother and I followed in a neighbor's car, and we could see paramedics pumping Huero's chest through the small am-bulance window. My mother screamed like she was being tortured. It was a real-life nightmare, worse than anything I ever dreamed. I shook off the memory, closed our blinds, and headed back to my room.

In the hallway, my mother had set up a tiny table beneath an old picture of Huero. Two red church candles were burning under the photo. I could see my brother's face dimly in the dark. It was like he was watching me.

"I miss you, little brother," I whispered to his picture.

The last time I whispered to Huero was on a night last spring. He had a bad dream, and he came into my room and woke me up.

"Martin, I'm scared," he said, his eyes half closed.

"Don't worry," I said to him. "Ain't nothin' in a dream that can hurt you." He yawned and rubbed his eyes. It was as dark and quiet a night as it ever got in our neighborhood.

He fell asleep next to me, and I was awake the whole night because he snored loudly and kicked me a few times. I was annoyed with him then, but now I'd do anything to have that time back. You're gonna have a moment like that too, a time when you wish for things to be back the way they used to be, even if they weren't perfect.

In the flickering candlelight, shadows crept up and down the hallway like ghosts. I remembered the boy I saw in the office at Bluford just before I passed out.

Was it Huero?

It might have just been the hit to my head. Maybe I was losing it.

Or maybe he was still with me somehow. Watching over me the way I was supposed to watch over him.

I'm so sorry I didn't protect you, little brother.

At 7:00 my alarm blasted me awake like it did every other morning. Only this time, I felt like kicking it. I must have slept an hour or two at most. The last place I wanted to go was Bluford High School.

Homework? I couldn't remember what my last assignment was even though it was just a day ago. When you're trying to survive, schoolwork is the first thing you drop. Teachers never seem to understand this.

On my way to school, I passed the parking lot where Frankie split my head open. Seeing it gave me the chills. And I got that gnawing feeling too, the one that tells you something bad is about to happen.

I looked around just to make sure Frankie wasn't following me. I kept picturing him standing at my front door, my bandana in his hand. The same hand that held a gun to my face. He wasn't anywhere in sight. Not yet.

At Bluford, I climbed the steps and noticed a few students looking at me funny. One kid was staring right at the stitches along my hairline.

"You got a problem, homes?" I said. The kid shook his head and walked away. "Yeah, that's what I thought."

Inside it got worse. It seemed everyone was secretly eyeing me as I walked down the hallway.

"Yo, that's the dude who got kicked out of his old school for selling drugs," someone whispered.

"Don't mess with him. He might be packin'," someone else mumbled.

Listening to them, you'd think I was one of the terrorists the FBI was always hunting. Rumors in school are like that, spreading like a fire no matter how false they are.

At my locker, I spotted someone familiar coming down the hallway toward me. Vicky. What was I going to do about her? With Hector and Frankie on the street, there was only one answer, and I hated it.

Vicky and me met my first day at Bluford. I noticed her the second I stepped into Mr. Mitchell's English class. He was in the middle of telling kids not to be late when I walked in with my attitude. My timing was so perfect that a few kids busted out laughing, and I played along. Vicky smiled, and when I saw her I almost forgot how angry I was that my mom had dragged me across the city to Bluford.

"Excuse me, sir, you have a guest," Steve Morris said, pointing me out to the teacher so he could get a laugh from his friends. I knew right then I didn't like him.

For a second, everyone stared at me like I was from another planet, like they never saw a kid from the barrio before. At Zamora High, almost everyone was brown like me. Bluford was the opposite, more black kids than anything else, although there were some Latinos, Asians, and a few white kids mixed in. If you ask me, Vicky's the finest Latina in the school.

I ended up sitting behind her and found myself daydreaming about her soft brown skin and the way her black hair spiraled down her back. Even her laugh sounded pretty. Like music, if you can believe that. My boys would never stop teasing me if I told them this.

"What's up with you, homes? You gettin' soft now that you're sweatin' that Bluford girl," Chago would say. It was true. Dude shouldn't talk, though. When his first girlfriend broke up with him, he got drunk and cried. I never told Frankie because he would have made a big joke out of it. He was cruel like that.

Mr. Mitchell put me and Vicky in a group to go over a homework assignment. We had to write an essay about heroes. Both of us ended up writing about someone in our family. Vicky wrote about her grandmother who died, and I wrote about Huero. I gotta admit it was the first time schoolwork ever helped me meet a girl. But it's true. When we read each other's papers, something clicked.

That Saturday, we spent the whole afternoon together. We walked in the park and grabbed some pizza. It was like one of those corny TV shows. But it was nice. For once, I wasn't the troublemaker who kept getting in fights, the son who almost hit his mom, or the thug about to throw his life away. Instead, I was Martin Luna, the person Vicky liked.

I had such a good time I felt guilty, like I was lying about who I really was. I even tried to tell her about it. It was the first time I was so honest with a girl.

"Vicky, you and me, we're different from each other," I had said, looking for the right words. "Really different."

"*So?*" she said. "What's that mean?"

"It just seems like you shouldn't be here with me," I told her. My face burned when I spoke. If she knew me and my homeboys were planning to shoot someone, she'd never even look at me. I hated being so dishonest, but how could I tell her the truth?

She touched my hand then, just for a half a second. My heart skipped.

"Martin, when I first saw you I was like, 'Oh no, who is this boy, acting so hard?' But when you wrote about your brother, you seemed so sad. That's when I decided I wanted to talk to you."

For an instant, I thought she was feeling sorry for me, and I nearly walked away just like that. I don't want any girl's pity. I ain't no one's charity case. But she stopped me.

"It's not like that," she said, pushing her hair behind her ear so she could focus on me. She rested her hand on her neck for a second. I couldn't take my eyes off her. "It's like you're more real than the guys around here."

I couldn't tell what was real anymore, but I knew I wanted her to always feel that way about me. And in a way, I understood what she was saying. Compared to other girls I knew, she was more real too. Deeper.

But who was I kidding? After what happened with Frankie, everything was different. We had to end things.

I took a deep breath as Vicky approached my locker. For the first time since we met, I didn't want to see her. Don't get me wrong. It's not that I don't like her. It's the opposite. I like her too much to let her get tangled in my mess.

"Martin!" she said, stopping just

behind me. "Are you okay? I can't believe you're back in school." I watched as she struggled not to stare at the stitches on my forehead. "I was so worried about you."

Her words burned my insides, like she was poking deep into my chest with a hot iron. Looking at her dark hair, her soft skin, and her concerned eyes, I knew I had to get her as far from me as possible.

Don't think I'm crazy. It's what I learned from Huero's death. If I'd kept him away from me and Frankie, he wouldn't have been on the street when the bullets were flying. It's a mistake I won't make again. The bandana on my door told me everything I needed to know. The only way to keep Vicky safe was to keep her away from me.

"I'm fine, Vicky. Just a little bump on my head. No big thing." I shifted my books and tried to hide what I was thinking. She stared at me oddly, her eyes intense and focused like twin spotlights on my face. I wished I could hide myself from her gaze, but there was nowhere to go.

"You scared me yesterday. All I could think about last night was your face and that cut on your head." She shook as if the image in her mind hurt her some-how.

"C'mon, Vicky. You know I'm hard-headed. It takes more than a little cut to keep me down." One of my books slipped out of my hand and slammed down to the locker floor with a loud crash.

Vicky jumped at the sound and took a deep breath. Overhead the first bell rang, and people in the hallway started rushing off. We had two minutes to get to class. Two minutes for me to force myself to act this way.

"What happened yesterday? You have to tell me."

"Just an argument that got a little out of hand. We're cool now, though," I said, picking up the textbook and trying to act calm. "It ain't nothin' to worry about."

She stepped back and cocked her head like I just insulted her. I pretended to organize some things in my locker.

"What's wrong with you, Martin?"

"*What?*"

"You're acting different."

"I'm sorry, Vick, but it's been a crazy time for me. There's just a lot of things I need to sort out right now."

"You wanna talk to me about it?"

I looked at her, and for a second I didn't know what to say. Of course, I wanted to talk to her. I wanted to listen to her, and part of me wanted to kiss her right there in the hallway.

But the best thing I could do was to get her to walk away from me, and the only way to do that was to make her want to leave. Asking her wouldn't work. She was too stubborn for that. I learned that when Steve Morris and his football player friends jumped me on the street.

"Just leave, Vicky," I told her when he and his boys climbed out of his car. "Go!" I yelled. But she didn't budge until my crew showed up and she knew I was safe.

It was all too close. She coulda been punched or stabbed or worse, and it would have been my fault. I couldn't live with myself if that happened. If it meant I had to lose her to protect her, so be it.

"We gotta get to class," I said, acting like she meant nothing to me.

Her jaw dropped.

"I don't understand. What happened to you? Did that bump on the head make you forget Saturday, you know, the day we spent together in the park?"

"I remember everything, Vicky. What do you want me to say?" I asked bitterly. "It's not like it was *that* special. It was just a walk, that's all," I lied. The truth was that it was the best day I had since Huero died.

Vicky shook her head at me.

I'm so sorry, girl, I wanted to say. *But it's for your own good. Frankie's coming. You gotta stay away from me.*

The second bell rang loudly. We had a minute to get to class. Vicky was never late before, but I could tell she would be today. It was all my fault, but what could I do?

"You're being such a jerk right now. What's your problem?"

I got more problems than you know, I wanted to say, but I bit my tongue.

"The only problem I have right now is you, Vicky," I said and turned away, hating myself.

I left her standing in the hallway alone.

Chapter 4

"It's about time, Vicky. I told you he's no good. I don't know what you saw in him in the first place," said Teresa, Vicky's closest friend. I could hear them talking in the hallway as we made our way to English class. Several hours had passed since I told Vicky off. They couldn't see me in the crowd behind them.

"You don't even know him—"

"I know he's nothing but a wannabe gangbanger, and that's all I need to know," Teresa said, cutting Vicky off.

Since we met, Teresa did nothing but give me dirty looks. I usually gave them right back 'cause I have no time for snobs.

"That's why he got beat up, 'cause he's a jerk and no one likes him," Teresa scoffed. "I guess he's not so tough if he got beat up that bad. You're better off without him."

I bit my tongue and kept my mouth shut, but it wasn't easy. If Teresa wasn't trying to cheer up Vicky, I would have told her off right there in front of everyone.

"Whatcha talkin' 'bout, Teresa?" cut in Roylin Bailey, a boy who sat in the back row near me in class. "I heard Martin clocked your boy Steve in Mr. Dooling's class. I'da paid cash money to see that," he added.

"Boy, you should save yo' money so you can buy some sense," said Tarah Carson, this heavy girl who knew everyone at Bluford. "Besides, it ain't none of your business, so just stay out of it."

"Can you *all* just drop it?" Vicky snapped as the group reached our classroom. I felt bad she had all this attention, but there was no way I could stand up for her. It would only make things worse.

"Drop what, Vicky?" asked Steve Morris. He came from the other side of the hallway and surprised her.

"Just forget it," she replied, rolling her eyes and darting into class. I was seconds behind them walking into the classroom.

Teresa was the first person to spot me entering. Her face twisted when our eyes met, like she just looked at a pile of garbage.

"Aw, c'mon, Vicky. Why you gotta be that way?" Steve said as I made my way to my seat. He glanced at me as I sat down, his eyes narrow and angry.

My problems with Steve started in gym class. I watched him slam into this short kid Eric who was playing him strong on the basketball court. Afterward, Steve boasted like he'd beaten Lebron James one-on-one. The rest of the class laughed along even though Eric was hurt. Just like at Zamora, it was the cowards who laughed loudest.

"It don't take much skill to hit someone half your size," I said, sick of listening to Steve show off. People in the locker room looked shocked, like I was supposed to be scared just because he's Bluford's star running back. Forget that!

The next day, Steve and his boys sucker punched me. I didn't even see them until I was on my back staring up at Steve's smirk. I couldn't let it end like that, so I followed him into the locker room and clocked him. That's when I got busted for fighting.

At first, no one told Ms. Spencer I hadn't thrown the first punch. But then Eric and Vicky came forward and told her the truth. Ms. Spencer kicked Steve and four other guys out of this week's football game. If you ask me, that ain't even punishment. Who cares about missing a stupid game?

But football's a big deal at Bluford, and Steve cared. The next day, he came at me again. Me and Vicky were walking down the street when this car whipped around. Next thing I knew, Steve and the four other guys surrounded us. It was five to one, and I was getting nervous, when Frankie and our crew pulled up in his LeMans.

"Hey, homes," Frankie barked as he got out of his car. "You ain't havin' a party without us, are ya?" He then spit a nasty white glob on the ground at Steve's feet.

Steve and his friends looked like they were about to wet their pants. It would have been funny, except Frankie had that sick smile on his face, the one that told me it was about to get ugly. He was going to put someone in the hospital—or a body bag. That's when I jumped in.

"He ain't worth it," I said, holding

Frankie back just long enough for Steve and his crew to get away. I knew things between me and Frankie would go downhill after that, but I just couldn't watch him ruin another kid, not in my name. Not after everything with Huero.

Steve wasn't about to thank me for saving his butt, though. I could see that in his eyes as I sat in Mr. Mitchell's class. Even though he was talking to Vicky, he was looking at me like he was planning something.

"Like I said, Steve, just drop it," Vicky replied. She started to look back toward me but then stopped herself.

Steve's jaw tightened up. His leg was twitching like he was ready to pounce. Up until I came along, he and Vicky were friends. They even went out for a few months last year. She told me it was no big deal, though Steve's eyes always said it was.

"Oh, so now you're not talking to me?" he asked, glaring at Vicky and then at me. "Don't tell me you're still into Sanchez. He's just gonna drag you down, girl. Like my grandfather used to say, if you lie with dogs, you're gonna end up with fleas."

"Awww *snap!*" Roylin shouted. "That's

46

cold, yo. He said Martin's got fleas!"

My blood started boiling. I was trying to hold on, to let it end this way so Vicky would move on. But I was having trouble. My fingers were purple from squeezing my desk.

"Don't do this, Steve," Vicky said.

"Do what? Tell the truth about your new boyfriend?"

"He's *not* her boyfriend," Teresa said. "She hasn't seen anyone since you two broke up."

"I don't need you to speak for me!" Vicky snapped, flashing an angry glare at Teresa.

"What's the matter, Vicky. You and Sanchez get in a fight?" Steve asked, a smirk on his face. "That must be where he got all them nasty bruises on his face. Or maybe those are flea bites."

I couldn't sit there anymore.

"You got somethin' you wanna say to me?" I asked, jumping out of my desk. My chair fell backward with a loud crash, but I didn't care. Teresa's jaw dropped like she'd witnessed a crime.

"You better be careful, *homes*," Steve replied, a smug grin on his face. "No one's gonna protect you in here. Not like last time."

Anger raced through my veins like fire. The truth was *I* protected *him* from Frankie. He knew it, but he was putting up a front, saving his reputation. I shoved a desk aside and moved toward him, my fists clenched, my pulse pounding like a drum in my forehead.

"Martin, don't!" Vicky yelled.

I ignored her. In my head, I could see myself smashing the smile off his mouth, breaking his nose. For a second, it was like the whole world had tilted, driving me toward him. Like he was the reason my life had fallen apart. Like hurting him would make it all better.

"*Martin!*" A deeper voice shouted, snapping me from my thoughts. It was Mr. Mitchell. He'd come into the classroom without us noticing. "Get back to your seat. *Now!*"

Dozens of eyes focused on us. Some people, like Vicky, were concerned. But most seemed hungry to watch a fight. You know how school is.

Steve stared at me with a cold, hate-filled smile.

"Whatever," I said. I walked back to my desk, grabbed my chair, and sat down. My ears were ringing and my hands shook with anger, but I held it in. Barely.

"I will see you after class, Martin," Mr. Mitchell said and then quietly began taking attendance. The class sighed, and people slowly turned to face the front of the room.

I took a deep breath, grabbed my notebook, and tried to swallow down the rage that still smoldered in my chest.

"Revenge is sweet," Mr. Mitchell said then, pausing so his words hung in the air. "Is this a true statement? Is revenge a good thing?" he asked, eyeing Steve, me, and the rest of the class. It was one of his trick questions. Everyone looked around for a second to see who was brave enough to answer. I didn't move.

"Definitely," Steve spoke up. That grin was on his face again. He even looked over at me. "If someone wrongs me, I'm gonna do what I gotta do to teach him a lesson."

"Okay," Mr. Mitchell replied. "I think a lot of people would agree with you, Steve, although Vicky doesn't appear to be one of them," he said turning to her. Her hand was raised, and she looked annoyed.

"But when does it end?" Vicky cut in. "I mean if someone does something to you, and you do something back. Then the person just wants to get back at you, and it goes on forever. How does that solve anything?"

Steve was silent for a second. "Hey, I'm just bein' real. That's just the way it is. If people can't handle it, they shoulda never started trouble to begin with," he said.

"But what if someone gets in your face when *you're* doing something wrong? Are you going to get revenge then when it was *your* mistake that started everything?" Vicky cut back, her words sharp as blades. Though she said no names, I knew she was talking about how I called Steve out for hitting Eric. "Oh, I forgot, *you* don't make mistakes."

Some students laughed. Even Steve smiled with a look that said Vicky proved her point. I loved seeing her in action. Her almond eyes were so intense you could almost feel heat from her stare.

"Easy, Vicky," Mr. Mitchell said. "What Vicky is showing us is that revenge can be messy. Very messy. What we are about to read in this class is a messy revenge story. One which involves lies, betrayal, violence, even murder—"

"Sounds like a day in the 'hood,"

Roylin said, and a few students laughed.

"Nope, it's *Hamlet*, a 400-year-old play that is as rough as anything we've seen in the movies or read in this class."

A few kids rolled their eyes as Mr. Mitchell started passing out books to each of us. *The Tragedy of Hamlet, Prince of Denmark* by William Shakespeare. I flipped through my copy. It was filled with old-fashioned words like in my mother's Bible. *Thou* and *thine*. Who can read that stuff?

The word *Hamlet* seemed stupid to me too. Like the name of a sandwich or something. But the way Mr. Mitchell described it made it seem interesting. A revenge story involving a murder. It sounded too familiar.

The next thing I knew, Mitchell had the class reading a scene out loud. There was this ghost of someone who had been killed. He was begging for his son Hamlet to catch his murderer.

"*Avenge me*," he said over and over again. Even though it was 400 years old, I knew the meaning of the words. I lived them every day when I thought about Huero and the coward who shot him.

At the end of class, I was reading ahead, slowly connecting the strange words like pieces in a large puzzle.

"Martin, what happened today?" Mr. Mitchell asked as soon as the class emptied. He closed the door so no one could hear us. His voice was almost angry. I didn't want to hear a lecture, not after Steve started with me. That boy was asking for it.

"Huh?" I said, playing dumb.

"Don't give me 'huh,' Martin. I'm done playing with you. You are skating on thin ice in this school—"

"*So*? You think I'm just gonna sit there and let someone diss me? That ain't hap'nin'."

"Martin, listen to me for a second. I'm talking to you man-to-man now."

"Oh, so now we're gonna be friends? Wassup, homes! Go ahead, Mr. Mitchell. Let's be *for real*," I snapped, unable to stop the anger spilling from my lips. I know it wasn't his fault, but I just couldn't take it. My mom, Frankie, Vicky, Steve, and now him. It was just too much.

"Martin—"

"What do you want me to say? *Sorry, Mr. Mitchell,* I was wrong to stand up in class. Next time I promise to sit there like a punk and let him bust on me," I said, checking my anger before it went too far. "Look, Mr. Mitchell. I gotta go."

He did something that struck me then, something that hurt.

His eyes dropped, his shoulders slumped forward, and then he nodded.

"Go," he said quietly. "Get out of here."

That second, he looked defeated. It was like I had truly exhausted him. I knew I was pushing him away, but I guess I was testing him, hoping he wouldn't give up, trusting that someone still believed in me. Anyone.

You are talented and have potential, Martin, he had said the other day. I held those words like a lifeline when Frankie was hitting me. They led me back to Bluford, made me contact Officer Ramirez, gave me hope that there was more for me than streets where brothers die.

"Maybe you were wrong about me, you know, what you said the other day." I could feel my anger thawing for a second, sense the ocean of sadness beneath it.

"No, Martin, *you* are wrong about you," he said, rubbing his forehead. "Wrong to blame yourself for things that aren't your fault. Wrong to keep pushing people away, wrong to let stupid comments from Steve jeopardize your career here at Bluford. Wrong to protect guys that aren't your friends."

I couldn't speak or move. My feet were nailed to the floor, and my mouth was glued shut. He was dropping truth on me like a rain of bombs.

"You're wrong about *me*, too," he added. "I'm not here to punish you or make your life difficult."

"I guess *you* got all the answers then," I replied, kicking my foot against my desk.

He took a deep breath. "No, I don't, Martin, but I know some of what you're going through. My nephew was killed by a stray bullet in a drive-by shooting nine years ago just a few blocks from this school. He was only six years old," he said resting his hand briefly on his chest like he was saying a prayer.

I couldn't believe what I was hearing.

"The police never found the person who did it, and to this day, I think it's because people are too scared to talk," he said.

I could feel him watching me. I kept my eyes focused on a crack in the tile floor. Anything to avoid his gaze.

"I'm sorry."

"I see too many kids taken down on these streets, Martin. Too many young people swallowed up by drugs, guns, and gangs. Kids who don't know better making bad choices that ruin their lives. I decided a long time ago to try to catch kids before they fall. It's one reason I became a teacher. I'm sayin' this so you know where I'm coming from in case you want to talk."

"You think I'm one of those fallen kids, don't you? That's why you're always in my face?"

"No, I think you've got a difficult choice to make. Right now, you're still standing. But if you get kicked out of this school, where will you be? Another fight and that's what will happen."

I glanced up at him. "School is the least of my problems."

He nodded. I could hear students lining up in the hall outside his door. His next class was about to start.

"Martin, we both know you know a lot more than you told the police the other day. As someone who has lost someone, I need to say this. For your brother's sake, you've got to tell the police what you know. I know it doesn't sound right, but if you keep one kid safe

55

because you get a gun or a criminal off the street, it's worth it."

Mr. Mitchell had been making sense until he started asking me to snitch on my friends. Then I started feeling pressure in my head. Like my skull was crammed full of tangled knots. I needed to get away from him.

"Next period is about to start," I said, getting up from my chair and heading toward the door. "I gotta go."

He sighed and followed me to the doorway. "Remember what I said, Martin. You have a choice to make. My door's always open if you ever want to talk."

I nodded and rushed past him into the crowded hallway, never looking back.

The last class of the day was gym with Mr. Dooling. Thanks to my doctor's note, all I did was sit on the bleachers and watch everyone play basketball. Steve, Clarence, and the rest of their friends dominated the court, but they weren't pushing anyone around, not even Eric. He nodded to me from the other side of the gym.

It was the first time I'd seen Eric

since my fight in the locker room. I wanted to smack him for talking to Ms. Spencer. Yeah, it was brave, and it got me out of trouble, but so what? Where I come from, talking to the principal could get you beat up—or worse. I couldn't handle him getting hurt for me.

"Eric," I said, walking up to him after class. "We need to talk, bro." He smiled when he saw me, a look that reminded me of my little brother. For a split second, I almost forgot what I was going to say.

"Wassup, Martin. You all right?" he asked, glancing at the cut on my head. "Man, what happened to your face? It wasn't Steve, was it?"

"Don't worry about it," I snapped, angry that he was still looking out for me. "Look, Eric, I heard about what you said to Ms. Spencer. You need to stay out of my business, homes. You hear me?"

"What's your problem? I just told her the truth."

"I don't care what you told her. Just stay out of it. What you did was stupid." I felt guilty saying the words. It was like back in the day when I scolded Huero for following me and Frankie. But if I'd only been harder on him, maybe he'd still be here today. I wasn't making that mistake again.

"*Stupid*? I was sticking up for you. The only thing that would be stupid is if I let you get busted when you didn't do nothin'. If you think that's the kinda friend I am, you got me all wrong." His brow was creased and his eyes were focused. He meant what he said.

That's what scared me. I couldn't handle another person being in danger because of me. Another person I might not be able to protect. The next thing I knew, I heard myself blurting out words I never meant, words I shouldn't have said.

"Who you kiddin', Eric? We ain't friends. You can't even take care of yourself, so you got no business worryin' about me," I said, giving him a shove to make my point. "From now on, just stay away from me, and stay out of my business."

"What's your problem, Martin? What'd I do to you?" he said, not even trying to defend himself.

I wished he'd insulted me or called me a coward for being too scared to be his friend. But he didn't. Instead he just

58

stood there, looking hurt and confused. I couldn't stand looking at him like that.

Without a word, I turned and stormed out of Bluford, glad to escape the place that felt more like my prison than my school. I'd only gone two blocks when I spotted something that made my heart drop to my feet.

It was Chago. He was watching me from across the street.

Chapter 5

"Yo, homes, wassup?" Chago said, lighting up a cigarette. His words seemed normal, but his face was pale and tense, like he was about to throw up.

I glanced up and down the block to see if he had come with Frankie, but there was no blue LeMans anywhere.

"Wassup, Chago," I said, eyeing him cautiously.

He took a long drag of the cigarette and blew a cloud of smoke into the air. I could smell the stink from across the street.

When we were kids, he and I used to hang out all the time. In junior high, we started messing around with cigarettes and beer like the older kids. I hated that stuff. The smell, the taste, the cost. But Chago was different. In eighth grade, he discovered weed, and for a while, that was all he wanted to do.

To pay for it, we stole things. A car stereo here, a bicycle there. No big deal, but it wasn't right. I remember how I had felt when Huero's bike got stolen, how I wanted to beat up the kid that did it. And then one day I became that kid. It's all ancient history now.

No matter what stupid things we did back in the day, me and Chago were always tight. He would always tell you what he was thinking straight up, and since he and I were cool, we never had any problems. Not like me and Frankie. You know all about that.

"Martin, we need to talk, homie." His voice sounded forced and unnatural, like someone had a knife stuck in his back.

"Tell me something I don't know," I replied, double-checking to make sure we were alone. "Where is he?" Chago knew exactly who I was talking about.

"He ain't here, Martin. Not yet," he said, crossing the street. "He doesn't know I'm talking to you, and to be honest, I can't believe I am either."

He tossed his cigarette butt onto the sidewalk, pulled out another one and fished around in his pocket for a lighter.

He smoked whenever he was nervous.

"Man, you keep smoking like that, and you're never gonna be an old man, Chago," I said. I knew how silly the words sounded, like the warnings you see on cigarette packs. When you're just trying to get through today, you don't even think about tomorrow. "Besides, you smell bad enough already without them nasty things."

He laughed, but there was nothing happy about the sound. Like the laugh you have at a funeral when you recall something funny about the person who passed away.

"Remember how we used to run up and down the street when we were kids? When playing was all we had to worry about?" Chago said, carefully putting the cigarette back into the box and kicking the curb with his shoe. I'd seem him do that a thousand times whenever he was thinking.

"Yeah, I remember. That was a long time ago."

"I wish we could go back there," he said.

"Me too, homes. I'd give anything just to go back to last summer."

Chago winced. I knew the words hurt

him. Of all my friends, he was the one who liked Huero most. He cried with me at the funeral, and he wanted revenge as much as I did.

"Frankie's pissed at you, homes," he said suddenly, changing the subject. "I ain't never seen him so mad."

I nodded. I expected as much. "I know. You think I'm stupid?"

"I don't know what to think about you anymore," Chago said with a sigh. "You used to be one of us, and now look at you. Frankie says you punked out and ratted on us to the cops, like you wanted us arrested or something. Ramirez been all over us for the past two days."

"Man, all of you been smokin' too much. You know I ain't like that. I never said Frankie or anyone's name to the cops. You believe me, right?"

Chago shrugged. I could see that Frankie had worked hard to turn him against me. "Then why did Ramirez stop by checking us out like we did something?" he asked.

"'Cause Frankie left his signature on my face. Ramirez ain't stupid. He knows somethin's up." Chago nodded. He knew I was telling the truth.

63

On the street, cars slowly passed by. One driver, an old white man, eyed us as he approached the corner where we were standing. He even locked his car doors as he waited for the light to turn, like we were carjackers or something. I almost said *Boo* just so he'd stop staring. Chago spat on the ground as the light changed and the car raced away.

"So that's it then? You just walkin' away from us and leavin' Hector on the street like nothing happened? What about Huero—"

"What *about* Huero, Chago? The bullet that killed him was meant for Frankie. If I had stayed away from him, Huero would be riding his bike right now, not lying in the ground," I said, forcing the tears back.

Chago wiped something from his eye. We were both quiet for several seconds.

"I understand you hurtin', bro. All of us are. That's why we gotta get revenge. C'mon, homes. Let's talk to Frankie. He'll probably be cool with you if you come around now. From what I hear, Hector's at his crib tonight. Tanner Street ain't that far away. Let's do this like we said back in the day," Chago urged. "Let's do it for Huero."

Chago's last words caught me like a nail catches your skin. He acted like killing was the best way to show respect for a kid who never hurt anyone, who smiled at strangers and felt sad whenever he saw a stray cat. That's not my brother's way. Huero wouldn't want me to shoot anyone. He wouldn't want me abandoning Mom and wasting my life in jail either. I figured this out one afternoon when I cut class to visit his grave. No matter what Chago, Frankie, or anyone said, I had to *live* for Huero—not kill for him.

"*I'm* takin' care of Hector myself, Chago. *My way.* I don't need you or Frankie's help to do it," I snapped. It was true, though I wasn't sure how.

"Homes, you ain't thinking straight. We been tight for years, so I'm gonna tell you straight up. If you walk away like this, you're gonna make Frankie an enemy, and you'll be alone against Hector," Chago said. "It's like a street fight. The dude in the middle gets hit from both sides. You can't survive that."

"Then I won't survive," I said. "We all gotta go sometime, Chago. At least I'll see Huero again."

Chago glanced at me and then

turned away. I'd seen him act this way before, when he disagreed with me but knew there was no changing my mind. Like when I stopped buying him weed 'cause I thought he smoked too much.

"Why don't you take off?" he said suddenly. There was something desperate in his voice. "You know, run away or join the army or something. Just until Frankie cools down. Those recruiter dudes are all over the place these days."

I almost laughed in his face at how crazy his words sounded. You gotta admit, it's a messed-up world when going to war is safer than staying home.

"I'm serious, Martin. Go away for six months, a year," he added, almost like he was begging me. Chago had never given me advice before. Usually he was asking for it about girls, or work, or dealing with his mom. Frankie and I used to tease him about it. But things were different now.

"I can't leave, homes," I said. My mother and I had already moved across the city. And at 16, I wasn't joining no army. Besides, I couldn't leave my mother alone, not after what she'd been through.

Chago was about to try and argue

with me. I could see it in his face, but I cut him off.

"So is Frankie comin' for me, Chago? Is that why you came down here?" I asked.

Chago reached into his pocket and grabbed the cigarette he'd just put away. I knew the answer before he opened his mouth.

"You know Frankie. He don't take 'no' from anyone."

For several minutes, we stood on the corner and said nothing. Chago finished his cigarette, tossed the butt onto the sidewalk and looked back at Bluford.

"And what about you, Chago? Will you be with Frankie when he comes?"

Chago shook his head and cursed under his breath.

"It isn't supposed to be like this. We're brothers," he said finally, sadness in his voice. "C'mon, Martin. You were always the smart one. Can't you think of some way out of this? At least try makin' it right with Frankie. Try talkin' to him."

"Look at my face, Chago. This is what happened last time we talked. I got nothin' to say to him."

Chago sighed and played with his lighter, making the flame flare up and die back. I almost felt bad for him, the position he was in. But that's the way the world is, puttin' you in bad positions and forcing you to make a move. Like Mr. Mitchell said, you have to make a choice.

No one ever said choosing was easy.

"He got your mom's schedule from his sister, Martin. He knows she's working late this weekend. Saturday night. That's when he's coming, when you're alone," Chago said, his eyes like storm clouds. "You didn't hear this from me." He turned and started walking back across the street.

Watching him, I knew Chago was still my homie. He made a choice by risking his neck to warn me. It was more than many people would have done.

"Thanks for coming down here, Chago," I said as he left. His head was down, his eyes low. He didn't once turn back.

From now on, I was on my own. And Frankie was coming.

My head was spinning as I made my way home. Frankie was going to make a lesson of me. In a way, he had no choice. Everyone would think he was soft if he allowed me to stand up to him. People would start talking. His reputation would suffer, and then younger wanna-be's would push and test him to get respect. I'd seen it before. He had to prove to the rest of our crew that there was no questioning him.

But how far would he go? At the least, he'd give me a beating I wouldn't be able to walk away from after a day. Maybe worse. I remembered the doctor's words just before I was discharged from the hospital.

"Another shot to the head could cause brain damage."

I knew what another fight with Frankie would be. More shots to the head. Harder ones.

"I ain't never seen him so mad." Chago's words echoed in my head.

This time Frankie would be more brutal than ever. I kept picturing the way he kicked the kid at that party. The horrible wet crushing sound it made. Frankie would give me the same treatment. No, he'd give me worse.

By the time I made it home, fear was digging at me the way rats clawed through the walls of our old apartment. My mother was still at work, and it was dead quiet as I walked in and locked the door behind me. From the shadows at the end of the hall, Huero smiled at me from his picture.

"I might be seeing you again soon, little brother," I said crossing myself the way we do in church.

Getting beaten isn't what scared me most. I'd been through that enough times as a kid with my father. Once, when my mother was pregnant with Huero, my dad got drunk and started swinging. She fell trying to get away from him, and I jumped in between them.

"Stop it, Papa! You're hurting her," I screamed.

He hit me so hard my teeth pierced my lip like glass ripping through an old trash bag. I was on the floor in a puddle of blood when he left in a storm of English and Spanish curses. That was one of the last times I saw him. Eight years ago, and I still have a scar on the inside of my lip from the stitches, his only lasting gift to me.

At the time, my mom called me her hero, saying I protected her and my brother. But she never understood that it was *fear* that pushed me, not bravery.

Fear that if I didn't act, I'd lose them. Fear that I'd fail to keep my mom and brother safe.

Huero's death made those fears real, turned them into wounds that hurt worse than any bruises Frankie could give and scared me more than any threats.

Pacing in my apartment, I felt these fears again, driving me like hunger. If Frankie was coming for me, if he was going to bring everything he had against me, I wouldn't survive. But there was something I needed to settle first. A problem that would make my life a complete failure if I didn't solve it. One that would turn me into a restless ghost if I died before I could finish it.

I looked at Huero's picture and knew where I had to go. It was not about Frankie or Chago or Bluford. It was about Huero and the person who shot him.

Time was ticking. Frankie was coming. Ramirez had done nothing. I needed to move while I still could. I needed to find justice for my lost brother.

The next thing I knew, my feet were taking me away from our apartment to the bus stop on our corner. Without a word, I boarded the bus to Tanner Street.

To Hector Maldenado's house.

Chapter 6

It was about 4:30, and the October sun was still high overhead when I stepped off the crowded bus onto Tanner Street.

I'd been to the neighborhood a few times before. Huero had one of his little league games with the Police Athletic League in a park just off Tanner Street last year. Ramirez was an assistant coach with the team. That's how he and my mother met. Huero played center field.

Frankie and I had also been through the area in his car a few months ago when we were looking for Huero's killer. Frankie said he had a girlfriend that used to live not too far from the park. I remember the conversation because it was funny.

"This girl was so fine, homes. But she was bad news too. She used to hide knives in her hair just in case," he'd said.

I laughed because Frankie had no room to say anyone was trouble. He was the one with the gun hidden under his seat.

"She had to be trouble to put up with you," I said at the time.

"It's true. If I had a daughter, I'd never let her near me," he said. "You neither, homes. You're a mess," he joked, gunning the LeMans back home.

Tanner Street was a lot like my old neighborhood. Just a 15-minute bus ride from Frankie's house, about 40 minutes from Bluford High, the area was all Chicano.

Small one-story stucco houses faced each other on both sides of the street, some with little gardens, a few with statues of *La Virgen*, the Virgin Mary. Many houses had iron bars on the windows too, just like our old place.

Leaving the bus stop, I spotted a mural on the side of a nearby garage.

Increase da Peace, it read in faded silver and black letters the size of a person's chest. Beneath the words, the artist added an image of a maroon lowrider cruising in the sun, chrome wheels sparkling like diamonds. Between the words and the car, two giant brown hands were painted as if they were coming together in a handshake. If you didn't know better, you'd think the neighborhood was safe, that peace was on the march.

But more recent than the mural were the gang tags painted on the walls of nearby buildings. One even covered a corner of the mural, an insult to the art and its message. I didn't recognize the name, but I knew it was a sign of who was in charge. Hector's house was up the street. My fingertips started tingling, and my palms got sweaty as I moved closer.

If my mother knew where I was, she'd never let me out of the house again. And if she had any clue what I was doing, the tears would be flowing down her face in full force.

"If anything happens to you, it will kill me, *mijo*," she'd wail.

Truth is, I didn't know what I was doing as I walked up the block. Dogs in houses on both sides of the street started barking at me. Brown kids with faces like mine stopped playing to look at me as I passed by. On a nearby porch, I saw an elderly couple watching me. They were all people who knew not to trust strangers walking in their neighborhood, but there I was.

Chago's words were ringing in my ear.

"The dude in the middle gets hit from both sides. You can't survive that."

But I couldn't stop myself. It was like I was possessed as I marched up the block and spotted the homies outside 2187 Tanner Street, Hector Maldenado's house.

There were four guys standing next to a blue Ford pickup parked on the street. Another dude was behind the wheel, and other people were in front of the truck, though I couldn't tell how many because the hood was up.

"Homes, you ain't never gonna get that thing to start," said one guy without a shirt. He had a beer in his hand and a tattoo of a spider's web on his right shoulder. I could see it from halfway down the block. He was my height but bigger and more muscular.

"Man, give César a chance. He fixed it last time."

"Yeah, but that was before . . . you know."

"Yo, why don't you shut up about that, man? Show some respect."

"Relax, homes. I'm just bein' real, that's all."

"No, you're bein' real stupid."

I was close now. Maybe about ten yards away. If they weren't all looking at the truck, they would have noticed me walking right up the sidewalk. I still don't know what I was thinking or planning to do. Just looking for answers. For proof. A reason.

Maybe I was looking for something else too. An ending. I don't know.

"Try it now," a voice yelled from the front of the truck.

The dude behind the wheel turned the key, and the old Ford came to life in a cloud of blue smoke that I could have hidden in if I were smarter or saner.

"I told you'd César would get it working. Your brother's still got his skills, Hector."

"That's 'cause I'm the one who taught him," came the response.

My heart was racing as I stepped closer. I needed to see their faces if it was the last thing I ever did. I was just ten feet away when I first heard foot-steps behind me.

"Yo, homie, whatcha looking for? I hope it's a bus stop 'cause this ain't your 'hood."

The whole crew surrounding the truck suddenly turned to face me.

"You know him, Hector?" the dude behind me asked.

Two guys came around from the front of the truck then. One of them, a stranger to me, was standing, wiping grease off his hands with a rag. The other appeared a second later in a wheelchair. I knew his face.

In my head, I was at that party again. I was watching Frankie lean over a guy who was on the ground, hearing the thud of his boot as it slammed into the poor dude's stomach, dodging the foamy vomit as it poured onto the floor at our feet. The guy had looked up at me a sec-ond before the impact. Burned his face forever into my mind. I'd seen it many times in nightmares since the fight, but it was never in a wheelchair. Never with legs so thin and weak.

"No, I don't know him," said Hector, the guy holding the rag. He stepped toward me. "You looking for trouble, homes?"

My eyes were still locked to that wheelchair. I nearly went down right there in the street.

Please tell me it's not true, I told myself. But in my heart I knew it was. No one could have walked away from what Frankie did that night. Me, Chago, and the rest of the crew knew it, but we never said anything. Instead, we pushed it back. Buried it.

But some things can't be buried.

For a second, I was frozen. Paralyzed. The answers I searched for since Huero's death came crashing through my skull like a gunshot. It started with César and Frankie talking trash at the party. Then Frankie took it too far. He crippled César with that kick. Hector wanted revenge. He came after Frankie and found him on my block.

But Hector's aim was off.

And bullets don't have names. They cut down anyone. Everyone. Even eight-year-olds who are in the wrong place at the wrong time.

My legs suddenly felt weak. My stomach started churning. Before me were Huero's killer and Frankie's victim. One boy dead. Another in a wheelchair. And for what? I wanted to scream.

For what?!

Respect? Revenge? *That ain't nothin'!* Neither could fix César's legs, bring Huero back, or empty the graves of all the fallen kids lying in them now.

The world was spinning, and I felt like it was about to fling me off like a piece of garbage. Another life lost in the barrio, just like my brother. Another world crumbled into dust.

"Are you high, homes? You musta got some bad weed or somethin'," the big guy said with a laugh.

"I don't like the looks of him. Is he packin'?"

In an instant, hands were all over me, searching for a weapon I didn't have, one I knew I couldn't use even if I held it in my hands.

"He don't even have any money. You know he's gotta be usin'," someone said.

I got shoved to the ground and landed on my backside in front of a group of guys who were my enemies but didn't know it. They were no different than my old crew, and one of them had suffered too, would suffer for the rest of his life from the looks of things.

It was all too much. I felt like a blister about to pop. I had to get away, or I was gonna lose it. But if I told them the truth about who I was, it would be the end of me.

"I'm lost," I said to them. It was all I could say.

"You damn right, you're lost. You're in the woods now, homes."

"Man, I told you he's high. *Vato loco*. Stay away from whatever he's smokin'!"

"Five-O," someone yelled then, and the crew backed away as a black and white police car pulled up next to us.

"Again? That's the second one today," someone else added. I knew the reason. It was because of what I told Ramirez. I was sure of it.

"Is there some kinda problem here?" I heard a different voice say, though from the ground I couldn't see much. Then a car door opened.

"No problems, Officer," the big dude said. "Hey, why don't you pick up our trash for us. This boy's as high as a kite."

I looked up to see a white police officer, maybe in his early 30s, sizing me up like I was a crime scene.

"You okay, son?" he said slowly like I couldn't understand him. "I see your eyes are red. Have you been smoking something I should know about?"

It was the same old deal with the cops in the barrio. Here they were in front of a killer and didn't know it. And here I was with my eyes red from tears, and I'm accused of using drugs. I've said it before, I'll say it again. The world is messed up.

"I just need to get home," I said.

"Let's take you to the station first," he said, helping me into the back of the police car. Funny how my first time in a cop car was the one time I hadn't done anything wrong.

The crew watched as the cop pushed me into the backseat. César had wheeled around close and studied me, his stare cutting me deeper than any blades.

Tears rolled down my face as the car started moving. The questions that had haunted me for months suddenly had painful answers.

"You sure you're okay, kid?" the officer asked, eyeing me in the rearview mirror.

I shrugged and stared out the window. There was no way I could tell him what was going on inside me, the sudden twisting I felt deep in my bones. Like

I was an old rag and someone was wringing me out, wrenching me from the inside.

"I don't know what you're hiding, but you're one lucky kid," the officer said. "We just increased patrols on this block this week. If you'da been here before today, no one would have found you."

"Yeah, I'm *real* lucky," I said wiping my eyes. I knew my talk with Ramirez was the reason the patrols were added, but I didn't say anything. The officer had probably saved me, but I didn't care. Sitting in the caged backseat of the police car, I didn't feel lucky or saved. I felt cursed.

Hours passed before my mother finally arrived at the station. By then, she was so upset that she could barely look at me.

"I don't know what to do with you anymore, *mijo*. My manager at work is upset with me because I keep leaving work early. And if I miss another day, we're gonna have trouble paying the bills. I keep praying, but I can't seem to get any answers," she said sadly as we walked into the apartment close to 10:00 p.m.

Just seeing her made me ache

inside, but I didn't have any words that would make her feel better. I didn't have any for myself.

She wiped her eyes and shook her head. I was standing in front of my bedroom door. I hadn't told her or anyone what I saw. How could I explain that I felt like a bomb had blown out all that remained of me after Huero's death?

My mom started praying then, turning to the candles and the picture of Huero.

I closed my bedroom door, shut out the lights, and felt hot tears crawl down my face in the thick darkness.

Chapter 7

Suddenly I was on my hands and knees.

Struggling. Unable to move. Something tight was looped around my neck.

I look down and see black cords stuck through my arms and legs. Holding them like chains. I look up and see a giant web. Like the one in the tattoo on Hector's friend.

I was caught in it.

Nearby are two bodies I recognize. Huero and César. But further out there are more. Countless others I don't know. An endless sea of bodies, gray and still in the dark. Their eyes are closed. But mine are wide open. We're stuck in the web together.

I try to free myself, but I can't move. There's no sky and no ground. Just *blackness swallowing us like the ocean.*

I scream but no sound comes from my mouth . . .

"Wake up, *mijo*. You're dreaming." Mom's words startled me out of my sleep.

I sat up and threw the blanket off my arms as if it was the web that held me. My T-shirt was soaked with sweat. My heart was pounding.

"What is it, *mijo*?" my mom asked, turning on the light next to my bed. "Are you okay?"

"I'm fine, Ma," I said, wiping my face and taking a deep breath. "Just a crazy dream."

She sat at the foot of my bed. Her tired, bloodshot eyes looked like two cracked windows. Since Huero died, she seemed ten years older. And my troubles only made her age faster.

Watching her, I wished I could stop the suffering I caused, go back and redo that night at the party, or change that afternoon last July when Huero died. Mr. Mitchell was right to talk about choices, but all the ones I made were wrong.

I'm so sorry I put you through all this, Ma. I wanted to say, but the words didn't come. Instead, I just looked at the clock to avoid her eyes. It was 3:33 a.m.

"You never smile anymore, *mijo*," she said then. "I hardly remember what your smile looks like."

"You neither, Ma."

She nodded and wiped her eyes.

"You're right," she said, putting her hand on my arm. "When you and Huero were babies, I swore I was going to give you both a better life than the one I had. Nothing was more important. Now . . . " she paused, tears slipping down her face. "I just think I failed you. Failed my two babies."

I couldn't stand to hear her blame herself for my mistakes.

"It's not your fault, Ma," I said, forcing myself to look into her weary eyes. "You weren't on the street with Huero that day," I said, feeling the sorrow in my chest. The guilt. "He was with *me*."

"No. Don't do that, *mijo*. I see you walking around with the weight of the world on your shoulders, blaming yourself. You're not a parent. It's not your job to keep your kids safe. That's a mother's job," she said.

I don't care what she said. I knew more than she did about what really happened to Huero, how I could have

87

prevented everything.

I hugged her then because I didn't know what else to do. She held me and cried, each tear burning my insides hotter than any fire.

"I'm sorry I snapped at you last night, *mijo*," she said finally. "I know you are missing Huero too. It's just that I get so worried."

"It's okay, Ma," I said. I felt so bad for her. She had no idea about Frankie's visit or the trouble that was brewing. And I didn't have the heart to tell her.

"Martin, listen to me. I know I yell at you a lot, but there's a reason for it. It's because I love you. No matter what you think you did or what you blame yourself for, know that I love you. There is nothing more important in this world to me than you."

I felt the tears in my own eyes then. Tears of sorrow and guilt. Tears of fear and worry.

"I love you too, Ma," I said. "No matter what happens."

She hugged me again, though I could see the concern on her face. Something about my words unsettled her. It almost felt like a goodbye.

Maybe it was.

Three hours later, I was walking to Bluford. I hadn't slept after the talk with my mother, and I couldn't stand laying in my bed and staring at the ceiling, my mind racing with images I wished I'd never seen.

César crumpled on the ground.

Huero bleeding in my arms.

Frankie's smirk.

I was so out of it when my alarm went off that I left home without a shower, without looking at the clothes I wore, without even grabbing my books. I just had to get out.

On the street, I followed a group of kids making their way to school. I could hear them talking about their classes, worrying about their grades, their homework assignments.

I know it ain't right, but I felt like slapping them because they were happy. Because they didn't look in the mirror each morning and hate what they saw. Because they could sleep at night knowing they hadn't destroyed their family. If I was Frankie, I would have done it.

At my locker, I was surprised to see Teresa standing there waiting for me. Her lips were tight, and she looked like

89

she was being forced to do something she hated.

"Aren't you at the wrong locker?" I said to her.

Teresa sucked her teeth and rolled her eyes. "I don't know what Vicky sees in you. But I'm here 'cause she's my girl," Teresa said. "She's done nothin' but stick up for you since you got here, and you went and hurt her yesterday. That ain't right."

I cringed inside at her words. I knew I deserved the mean look she gave me, and I respected her for having the guts to stand up for her friend. She was right. Vicky did deserve better. That's why I pushed her away.

"I told her what she needed to hear," I said.

"No, you didn't. You were a coward who didn't even tell her anything. You need to step up and end it with her, so she stops worrying that there's something wrong with you. Just tell her it's over and show her what a jerk you are so she can move on."

I hated Teresa's voice, her attitude. The look in her eyes that told me she thought I was beneath her. But there was truth in her words that stung me.

Coward. Maybe I was afraid of being honest with Vicky. Afraid of what she'd really think if she knew what I was about. But even if it was true, it was none of Teresa's business.

"Girl, get outta my face. You don't know nothin' about me," I said reaching into my locker and grabbing my copy of *Hamlet.*

"I know you're the worst thing that happened to her. That's all I need to know," Teresa cut back.

I slammed my locker shut and headed down the hallway. I was supposed to go to biology, but I couldn't stand the idea of sitting in the class and talking about plant cells. What's the point of that?

Instead, I snuck into a far corner of the library behind the magazine racks and the computer tables. Another student bundled in a thick black jacket was asleep at a work table. I ignored him, grabbed a chair, and cut my next three classes.

During the time I cut biology, homeroom, and U.S. history, I read *Hamlet* and learned how he goes nuts planning revenge on his dad's killer, and then starts talking to himself and snapping at everyone around him. He even chases away the sad girl that likes him. I swear, it was like the play was talking about me.

I read so much, I decided to go to English class. As soon as Mr. Mitchell walked in, he announced a pop quiz.

"I hope everyone read the first act of *Hamlet* for homework," he said as he passed the quizzes out.

"Come on, Mr. Mitchell," Roylin complained. "Why you always gotsta do this to us?"

"If you know he always does it, it shouldn't be a surprise to you," Steve said. "Even Martin can figure that one out."

"Enough," Mr. Mitchell said. "No more talking until the quizzes are done."

Vicky turned and handed the quiz back to me. Our eyes met for a second. I wanted to talk to her, to explain, but I couldn't say anything. Not with Mr. Mitchell watching us.

The *Hamlet* quiz was easy. For the first time I could remember, I had no problem identifying who everyone was and what happened in the first act. In fact, I was the second person to finish the quiz.

"You okay, Martin?" Mr. Mitchell asked when I handed my paper in. "You sure you don't want to look over it again?"

A few kids snickered, like they couldn't believe someone like me could get the right answers. I looked back to see who was laughing, but no one met my gaze.

During the rest of class, I stared at the back of Vicky's head and tried to listen to Mr. Mitchell's talk about how guilt destroys Hamlet. But all I kept thinking about what was coming, what I still had to face.

Before class ended, I scribbled a note just in case.

Dear Vicky,

You're right to be angry at me. Right to think I'm a jerk.

I'm dealing with a lot right now, and I'm not sure how it's all going to turn out.

I didn't want to drag you into all my problems, so I thought the best thing I could do was push you away. I never meant to hurt you. Our walk in the park was the best day I had since I came here. Your smile kept me going.

Martin

P.S.—Teresa may be a jerk, but she's got your back. If you see Eric, tell him I'm sorry.

I folded the note, and dropped it on Vicky's desk without a word. It was the last thing I wrote in Mr. Mitchell's class.

Just a few hours later, my time at Bluford ended.

Chapter 8

"Get off!"

I could barely make out the words over the noise of showers spraying and locker doors slamming. It was the end of gym class, and I was emptying out my locker when the voice spoke out from the back of the room.

"Let go of me!"

This time I knew who it was. Eric. Then I heard people laughing and a low thud.

I rushed out into the aisle that divided the locker room. Our gym teacher, Mr. Dooling, was on the far end talking to a couple of football players. I could tell they were trying to distract him.

The air was a soupy mixture of steam, sweat, and deodorant. It was the last class on Friday. Most students were rushing to get changed and go home, but a few stood nearby looking toward the back of the locker room. No one moved closer, though.

Cowards. I cursed under my breath.

I knew whose lockers were there. It was where I'd fought Steve after his boys jumped me. I dropped my gym clothes and headed straight back. I could hear voices growing louder as I got closer.

"I told you to keep your mouth shut, Eric. Next time you want to be a hero and step up for your boy Martin, you better think twice. 'Cause if you ever rat us out to Ms. Spencer again, it'll be the last thing you do. You hear me?" I recognized the voice. It was Steve's friend Clarence, a linebacker on Bluford's football team, whose neck was as thick as a tire.

I stepped into the corridor and found Eric doubled over. Two guys had his arms hooked behind his back, the same two guys who had grabbed me from behind last week. Clarence was in front of them, and I watched his big dumb fist fly into Eric's stomach. Steve was on the other side of them, looking down on Eric, who coughed and slumped to his knees. I could see tears in his eyes as he looked around desperately for help.

"I got kicked out of this week's game because of what you said to Ms. Spencer. You better hope this doesn't affect my scholarship chances, or you won't walk again," Steve hissed, spitting on the ground.

That's when I snapped.

Steve's threat and the sight of Eric slumped over sent me flying out of control like a train off its track. I slammed my fist like a hammer into Clarence's chin. Steve gaped in surprise when I turned and jabbed his nose, knocking him backward into the wall of lockers. The two punks holding Eric let go and stepped back, eying me like I was a dog ready to tear into them.

"*Fight!*" someone screamed.

Clarence came at me then, and I started swinging, cursing, kicking. Everything seemed to go by in slow motion, but I kept thrashing even after the teachers arrived.

I couldn't explain why I swung at every arm that tried to pull me away. Why I was unable to calm down as they yanked me out of the locker room. Why I shoved poor Mr. Dooling against a wall when he tried to break my grip of Clarence's neck, or why I fought the three security guards who raced into the locker room and wrestled me to the ground.

Everyone—teachers, students, guards, even the janitors—stared at me like I was a monster with horns growing out of my head.

"Psycho," Clarence said, rubbing his jaw as I left the locker room.

"You're *done*, Sanchez," Steve yelled with a cold smile on his face. "Outta here. Have fun in juvee."

"He's lost it. That boy is nuts," one guard mumbled as they dragged me down the hallway like I was some kind of criminal.

"Maybe he's strung out on something," another guard said.

I know it must have looked that way. I was trembling and shaking. My jaw locked shut, my pulse pounding, sweat dripping off my face.

There was no way I could tell them that seeing Eric on the ground reminded me of my brother. No way I could describe the white-hot rage that boiled in my chest at them. There were no excuses for what I did. But in that moment, there was no way to hold it back.

Spencer's office, my head down on the same desk I sat in during my first suspension. My heart was still pounding, but the red haze in the air was disappearing like morning fog.

My eyes were wet and puffy. I must have been crying, and my hands were marked and swollen with cuts from the punches I'd thrown. My T-shirt was torn too.

Ms. Spencer came carrying a thick folder with my name on it. She sat down on the opposite side of the table from me. The lines in her forehead seemed even deeper than usual.

"I'm sorry I lost it, Ms. Spencer," I spoke up first. What else could I say to her? It was the truth.

She opened the folder, leafed through some sheets and then looked at me. It seemed like a long time before she said anything. "I'm sorry too, Martin," she replied.

Outside I could hear one of the secretaries talking to someone.

"A troublemaker like that doesn't belong in this school. I wouldn't want my child in class with a boy who behaves like that. Someone could have really gotten hurt today."

"I knew he was trouble the second he walked into this school. He was nothing but attitude from day one," another woman replied.

I wanted to jump up and tell them off. What did they know about me? Nothing. Sure, it was wrong to lose it in school. But what about ganging up on another kid when no one is looking? Which was worse?

If you ask me, it seems most people don't know what really goes on in school. And if they did, a lot more of the kids would be in trouble. Popular kids, not just the ones everyone thinks are troublemakers.

"Martin," Ms. Spencer said, her voice heavy and slow. "You are in serious trouble for what happened today."

I nodded. At least she was being straight up with me. "I didn't mean to push Mr. Dooling, Ms. Spencer," I admitted right away. "I'm sorry I did that. It should have never gone that far."

"Well, it's good to hear you say that. And I'll be sure to mention it to Mr. Dooling, Martin. But what happened today is . . . there just isn't much I can do for you. My hands are tied."

"What do you mean?"

She took her glasses off and stared at me. "Martin, you've been in this school for only two weeks. In that time, you've been suspended. You've cut class several times. You've been involved in multiple fights, and today, you struck a teacher. It took three guards to bring you here. I can't have that behavior in my school. Parents, teachers, and my staff will not stand for it, and neither can I."

"I said I'm sorry. Look, I was standing up for Eric. They were hitting him. What was I supposed to do? Leave him by himself to get beat up? I couldn't do that, Ms. Spencer."

She wrote some notes on a pink piece of paper. "This isn't the street, Martin. It's a school, and it has rules which you broke. I warned you last time about controlling yourself, and today you were worse than ever. I'll look into what happened, but that does not change what you did today or what I must do now." Ms. Spencer dropped her pen, put the pink sheet into my folder and closed it quickly.

"What do you mean? What's gonna happen?"

She took a deep breath and studied

my face for several long seconds. It was like she was looking for something to make what she had to say easier. "I hate to have to do this, Martin. To you and your mother," she began.

"What about my mother? What is it?"

"I'm afraid you are being expelled."

"*Expelled*? You mean you're kicking me out?" I asked, surprised at how much her words hurt.

She nodded heavily. "I'm very sorry, Martin."

I slumped back in my seat. The office was quiet for several seconds.

"Martin—"

"No, forget it, Ms. Spencer. It's all good," I said, trying to pretend I didn't care, but my voice was cracking. "I never belonged here anyway. Besides, I'm sick of you all gettin' on my case all the time. At least now I won't have to hear Steve anymore neither."

"Martin, listen to me," Ms. Spencer urged, leaning forward toward me. "Every student who is expelled is given a hearing in front of Mr. Gates, the superintendent. Yours will be next week. Go to the hearing, and explain your side of the story. Maybe you can convince him to allow you to remain at Bluford. But for now, I have to follow school policy. There's nothing more I can do."

If I got the news a month ago, I would have been happy. I never wanted to come to Bluford in the first place. But deep inside I could see it gave me a chance I didn't have anywhere else. And then there was Mr. Mitchell and those words.

Potential. Talent. Promising future.

Getting expelled was like saying there was no hope for me. That my place was on the corner with the other guys who were being gunned down and who were doing the shooting. Even though it wasn't cool to say it, I started wanting more than that.

Too bad, Martin Luna. Now you're going back where you belong, Ms. Spencer seemed to say.

She's right, homes. Stop pretending you're somebody else. School's not your world. You belong with your family, Chago would say. But I'd burned that bridge, too. My world was collapsing. The end was coming.

"Yeah, I'll talk to him, Ms. Spencer. I'm sure he's gonna listen to what I have to say. Just like everyone else around here," I said.

"Good luck, Martin," Ms. Spencer said with a weak smile. She wiped her eyes quickly and stood up.

I rushed out the front doors of Bluford High School for the last time, trying my best to hide the burning in my eyes. The angry tears that dripped down my face because another door had just slammed in my face.

It felt like a kind of death sentence.

Chapter 9

"*Expelled!*" my mother cried when she got home from work that night. I didn't even try to defend myself 'cause I knew there was no point. She wasn't going to listen to anything I had to say.

"I'm sorry, Ma."

"*Sorry?*" she yelled, her voice rising even higher, piercing my skull. "Is that all you have to say? That's not good enough. Sorry doesn't fix anything!"

"What do you want from me? I told you—"

"*What do I want?*" she repeated, cutting me off and moving right into my face. "What I want is for you to stop throwing your life away. Your principal told me you pushed a teacher. I couldn't believe my ears. 'Not my son,' I started to tell her, but she said at least ten people watched you do it. *Pushed a teacher!* Even at Zamora you never did nothin' like this!"

"Ma, I was standing up for my friend," I tried to explain. I needed her to understand that I wanted to do the right thing. That I didn't mean for this to happen. That no matter what happened, I wasn't a bad person. "I just lost it when—"

"Yeah, you lost it all right. You threw away everything. *Everything!*"

"Ma, you don't understand—"

"No, *you* don't understand. You're killing me! I can't take it no more. Everyday I go to work, I'm scared of what you're doing. Whenever the phone rings, I'm afraid to pick it up. One day you're in the hospital. The next you're in a police station. Then I get a call from your principal saying you got expelled. What are you trying to do to me?" she demanded, her words hitting me harder than any punches, breaking me up inside.

"But Ma, I told you it was an accident. I didn't mean to hit him. These dudes were hurting this kid and—"

"I don't want to hear it! I'm tired of you making everything so difficult all the time. And I'm tired of your excuses. No matter what happened, you could've handled it differently. Told a teacher. Talked to the principal. You had a choice. But what did you do? You went and started hitting."

I knew part of what she said was right, but she didn't understand what seeing Eric did to me. How it scraped open the wound of Huero's death. I was drenched in gasoline, and it was the match that set me on fire.

"I can't keep doing this, *mijo*. I'm getting too old," she said, heading down the hallway to her bedroom. Her voice became weaker somehow, like something deep inside her had broken. Had finally started to give up. "I moved us here to get you out of the barrio, to get you a decent education, and to give you a chance your brother will never have. If all you're gonna do is throw it away, shame on you," she said, taking a deep breath and wiping her eyes. "I need to go to bed. It's been a long day."

She walked past me into her bedroom and closed the door, leaving me standing at the edge of the dark hallway alone.

The candles beneath Huero's picture

cast the only light in the hall. I looked at his portrait and fought back the tears.

"I'm sorry," I whispered. To my mother. To Huero. To everyone I'd wronged.

But my mom's words echoed in my head, slicing me like switchblades inside, cutting me to the bone.

You're killing me . . .

Shame on you.

The words hurt so much I almost didn't care that Frankie was closing in like a pit bull ready to bite my throat.

Mijo,

I'm working late tonight for inventory. There are leftovers in the fridge. Nelson will bring me home. Call me if you need anything.

I reread the short note my mother stuck on our refrigerator. Her words were cold and distant. I crumpled the paper and tossed it in the trashcan when I heard a knock at the door.

For a second, I imagined Frankie had come already. But when I looked through the tiny peephole, I saw Vicky staring back at me. She looked nervous. Suddenly I was too.

I thought about not answering the door. It was almost noon, and I hadn't even showered. I knew I looked bad, but I couldn't just leave her standing there. And part of me was grateful to see her.

"Wassup, Vicky," I said, opening the door. She was wearing a snug pink T-shirt and jeans, and she looked better than ever. Seeing her, I didn't know what to say. My tongue was all in knots. All I could do was be honest. "It's good to see you, girl. I can't believe you came here, though."

"You think you're going to keep me away with a note like this?" she replied with a smile. She was holding the note I wrote her in class yesterday. "When I read it, I was like 'Why hasn't he just been honest with me?'"

She was staring at me, her eyes friendly and sincere. In her gaze, I felt exposed somehow. It was like she could see right into me. Like she was looking at the guilt in my heart, the stupid mistakes I made, the trouble hanging over me like a curse.

"Look, I'm sorry, Vicky. I've just had a rough time lately. A lot of stuff has been going on, and I didn't handle it well," I admitted. I needed her to understand I never meant to hurt her. "I shouldn't have treated you that way."

"You're right, and if you do it again, you'll be sorry," she teased.

"I *am* sorry, Vicky. Seriously," I said.

"I know you are, Martin. That's why I'm here," she replied. "You think I'd come over here if I thought you were a jerk?"

"Girl, you're crazy. Just because I'm sorry doesn't mean what I said to you isn't true. You should stay as far away from me as possible." I meant the words, forced them out even though they hurt to say.

"Oh my God, I am *sooo* sick of hearing that. Look at me, Martin. I'm standing here because I like you. If you honestly don't want me around, just tell me, and I'll leave. But if I hear another person—especially you—tell me I'm doing the wrong thing, I'm gonna freak."

"How can you be so sure about me, Vicky?" I said, unable to hide the sadness bubbling inside me. I stepped away from the door so I could hide my eyes, but she followed me.

"'Cause if you were really a jerk, you wouldn't try so hard to protect me, Martin," she said, putting her hand on my shoulder. "If you were really a jerk, you wouldn't have stood up for Eric in the locker room. And if you were really a jerk, you wouldn't apologize to me neither. Believe me, I know what I see in you, and I'm sure I'm right."

I felt like someone who had been lost in the desert. Her words were like water. I wanted to drink them in, to believe them, but I knew better.

"But there's so much you don't know, Vicky." I was staring at the floor, shaking my head. Snapshots of all the things I'd screwed up flashed through my head. Huero lying on the ground. Frankie kicking César. Me hiding the truth from everyone.

"So tell me! That's what friends do, right?"

We were standing in my living room. The sun was shining outside, and there before me was this beautiful dark-haired girl who challenged me like no one else. I looked at her and just shook my head. I felt like I was standing on the edge of a cliff, and she was asking me to climb down to the bottom with her. My heart was racing. "I don't even know how, Vicky."

She glanced over my shoulder to the hallway. I knew she could see the candles and Huero's picture in the distance.

"Is that your little brother?" she asked, slowly stepping past me toward the hall.

"Yeah, that's Huero. The picture was taken about a year before . . . you know." I moved next to her, our shoulders touching.

"Oh my God, Martin. You two have the same eyes."

"You think so?"

"Definitely," she said, examining the picture. "He's cuter than you, though."

I almost smiled at her then. "He was the coolest kid, Vicky. You woulda loved him." It was the first time I'd ever really talked about Huero to someone that didn't know him.

"I believe it," Vicky said. "I feel like I know him a little bit through you, and I like him already." She smiled and placed her hand on my shoulder.

I felt like I was melting inside. Like my anger and sadness was a tight fist that she was gently opening.

"I miss him so much," I confessed.

She rubbed my back then, and I couldn't hold back. It was like cracks were opening inside me and pain was ready to pour out.

"Why couldn't I have protected him? Why did he have to die, Vicky?" My voice was shaking, breaking up, but the words kept coming. "Why wasn't it *me* that got shot?" I asked, trying to pull away from her. But she held me.

"I'm so sorry, Martin," she said, pressing herself into me. There were tears in her eyes.

"It should have been me," I said, my face burning with shame. I had never said the words, but they haunted me every day. Clouded everything I did since Huero died. Made me hate my own reflection and wish I'd never been born.

"No, Martin," she said, touching my face. "It shouldn't have happened to anyone. Not you. Not Huero. But you can't do that to yourself. You have to go on. That's all we can do."

"It *should* have been me," I repeated, tears rolling down my face, my chest beginning to heave. I didn't want to cry. I had fought it for so long, kept everything buried down deep. But Vicky's words, her touch, and her tears thawed me. "I wish it was me. . . ."

I wept then like a small child, felt the hurt like lead weights on my back begin to lighten slightly. Vicky hugged me the

113

whole time. I listened to her breathing and felt her heart beat against my chest. Twice she wiped her own eyes, the tears she shed for Huero. For me.

I don't know how long we stood there holding each other in front of Huero's picture. When we finally pulled away, my T-shirt was splotchy and wet from our crying. With anyone else, I would have been embarrassed, but not with her. We stared at each other for several long seconds without a word. Then she did something that surprised me.

She leaned forward and kissed me.

Her lips were soft and smooth. I closed my eyes and touched her soft face, ran a hand through the long spiral curls that stretched down her back, smelled the strawberry shampoo she had used to wash her hair.

We kissed just once, but we spent the rest of the day together. I didn't tell her about César or that Frankie was coming later that night. I was afraid she might do something crazy and get herself hurt for me. I couldn't risk that.

"You have to fight your expulsion, Martin. You have to go to that hearing and tell the superintendent everything," she said later that day when we were eating pizza at Niko's.

"There's no way he's gonna listen to me. Everyone who saw me thinks I'm a thug. I heard the secretaries talking about me in the office."

"Who cares what they think? They don't get it. You gotta make them understand and show them who you really are," she urged. There was this tiny crease in her forehead. I'd seen it in class whenever she said something she really believed in. Now it was there because she believed in me. I didn't agree with a word she said, but I wanted to kiss her again right there. She was as much a fighter as anyone I knew, and she was on my side.

"But it's not that simple, Vicky," I explained. She started shaking her head at me. I know she didn't understand what it was like to have everyone think you were a criminal, how you were guilty before you even opened your mouth. "Besides, I pushed Mr. Dooling."

"Well, if you don't fight this, shame on you 'cause I expected more from you," she said, putting her hands on her hips. I couldn't believe her words. The same ones my mother had said.

"Girl, this isn't even about you. Why

115

are you getting in the middle of it?"

"I am already in the middle of it. Steve's my ex-boyfriend, remember? And then there's you." She smiled, and for a half second she blushed. She knew what I was going to ask her next. I could see it on her face.

"And what am I?"

"That depends. What do you want to be?" she asked with a sly smile. My heart jumped. I grabbed her hand.

For the first time at Bluford, I had a true friend. And for the first time in my life, I had found a girl who moved my soul. It figures both came on the day I had to face Frankie. The day after I was kicked out of Bluford.

"I'll tell you later," I said, holding her hand, making a silent promise to answer the question if I ever got the chance to be with her again. If I survived my clash with Frankie.

She squeezed my hand back and smiled. She knew I wasn't telling her everything, but right then it didn't matter. I wished I could have bottled the moment. Saved it forever somehow. Because at that table in the back of Niko's, with Vicky's soft hand in mine, I felt something new. Something I'd lost months ago, maybe something I never really had.

I felt glad to be alive.

And yet, even then, I could feel Frankie coming to strip it all away. Snuff it out like a candle.

If there was going to be any hope for me in this world, I had to stop him.

Tonight.

Chapter 10

Alone in the apartment, I paced for several hours hoping what Chago said was wrong. That Frankie was not coming for me, and I wouldn't have to see him again.

At 10:00, after checking and rechecking each noise and every car on the street, I turned out all the lights. Maybe Frankie would leave if he thought no one was home. Or maybe the crew would convince him to grab some beers and chill somewhere.

But deep down, I knew I was kidding myself.

"*I ain't never seen him so angry.*" Chago's words echoed in my mind.

I had to face Frankie one last time. It was the only way I'd be able to look at myself in the mirror, silence the angry voices in my head, and honor my fallen brother.

By 11:30, the apartment was still quiet. I stretched out on my bed listening to the sound of each car engine outside.

Each siren racing off in the distance.

Each rustle of the restless mice in the walls.

Only the red numbers on my alarm clock and the flickering candles under Huero's picture kept the place from being as dark and quiet as a grave.

As my eyes grew heavier, I started thinking Chago had managed to talk some sense into Frankie. Told him to leave me alone, to let it all go. I was almost nodding off when I heard the step outside our apartment door creak strangely.

If it were my mother, I'd hear keys jingling, the locks opening with a solid click. Not this time.

First someone tried to open the front door of our apartment. Of course, I had locked it, but Frankie knew how to break a lock just as fast as he could break a nose. There was a heavy thud, then a pop followed by a quick metallic snap. A second later, I heard the familiar groan of the door opening.

My heart started pounding like a bass drum. My palms grew slick with sweat. I grabbed Huero's old bat and crept out of bed to the edge of the doorway, careful not to make a sound. The door was half open, so I hid myself behind it and peered through the tiny gap along the door frame.

I could hear footsteps getting closer. From the sounds, I guessed at least three people had entered the apartment. Maybe more.

My worst fears were coming true. Frankie had brought the crew with him. My boys from back in the day—Jesus, Junie, and Chago—were now my enemies, breaking into my house in the middle of the night like thieves. Allowing Frankie to push them too far.

They paused for a second in our living room and whispered. In the silence, I could make out Chago whispering.

"I don't like this. That's Huero's picture on the wall. This ain't right."

"You scared, homes?" Frankie challenged. I knew his voice anywhere. "You back out now, and the scariest thing you'll see is me."

"I don't think anyone's here, Frankie." I recognized that voice too. It was

Junie, a dude who usually spent Saturday nights smoking weed, not hunting friends.

"Check the bedrooms." Frankie ordered. He was always getting people to do his dirty work. A year ago, he would have sent me to check the rooms, and I would have listened. No more.

My hands were tingling. I needed to stop him somehow. Stop him before he stopped me. I prayed my plan would work.

Our apartment was small. Only about twelve feet separated the front door from my room, and I could hear someone coming forward.

I gripped the bat tight, feeling the sticky tape Huero had put on it last spring.

The floor outside my room groaned slightly as someone approached. Then I heard footsteps move into my mother's room. Through the tiny crack in the door, I could see the back of a figure standing in the hallway looking at Huero's picture.

I raised my bat. The person stood still for several seconds, took a deep breath, and pushed open my bedroom door.

It was Chago. In the candlelight, I could see his eyes glistening and wide open with fear. He was staring right at me like he'd seen a ghost. If it was anyone else, I would have swung the bat, but instead I raised my finger across my lips so he knew to keep his mouth shut.

"No one's in here," whispered Jesus from my mother's room.

"No one's in here either," answered Chago, looking right at me. I thought his whisper was too quick. Too forced. He turned and headed back to the living room, leaving the door slightly open.

I knew Frankie would break him if he found out about the lie. Chago knew it too. His forehead was covered in a thin layer of sweat that reflected dimly in the dark.

"You sure the place is empty?" Frankie asked, frustration in his voice. I couldn't see what he was doing, but I could picture him scowling at Jesus and Junie, making sure he could trust them.

"There ain't no one here. Let's get outta here before his mom comes back." Chago said. Someone struck a match then. Chago was smoking. I was sure of it.

"Why you in such a hurry, homes?" Frankie asked. I could hear the distrust in his voice. I knew what it meant.

The apartment got dead quiet. Frankie was whispering, but he kept his voice low this time. I couldn't understand a word he said.

"I told you he's not in there," Chago yelled suddenly from the living room. I bet he was trying to warn me.

Then I heard footsteps rushing down the hallway.

I knew I was in trouble. My arms were trembling with nervous energy. I said a silent prayer and peered through the crack in the door.

In the flickering candlelight, I could make out half of Huero's picture, but there was something unusual about it. A reflection of dim figures in the area under Huero's face.

The one in front was definitely Frankie. I could see his torso and head suspended in the air. As the reflections grew bigger, I saw something shimmer just for a second. Something metal.

It was like Huero was trying to protect me somehow.

I stepped back and raised the bat, knowing where I had to aim. Frankie's right arm. He was just outside my door. Only a few feet separated us.

All was quiet for a second. I crossed myself.

Then chaos.

The door smashed inward as Frankie kicked it with his steel-tipped boots, the same ones he used to cripple César.

I swung Huero's bat with all my might.

It sliced through the air with a deep, hungry *whoosh*, sailing toward Frankie's outstretched arm. I saw the pistol in his hand glimmer for a split second as the bat came crushing down.

Boom!

The air exploded with a blinding flash and the thunderous crack of a gunshot.

In the blast, quick as a lightning strike, I saw the bat crumple Frankie's right arm, bending his trigger finger backwards like a snapped pipe.

Then the room filled with the sour sulfur odor of gun smoke. My ears rang from the blast, but I still heard Frankie's screams, a sound that made the dark room seem like a torture chamber.

"My arm!" he hollered, rolling on the floor at my feet. "I can't move it."

I turned on the light, the bat still in my hand. Frankie's gun was on the ground next to him. I kicked it away as he struggled to get up. A hole in the floor next to my bed showed the harmless path the bullet took.

Chago, Junie, and Jesus were at the edge of the hallway. They looked stunned at the sight of Frankie holding his arm and me standing over him with a bat. Their world was suddenly turned upside down.

"You know what you gotta do," Frankie grunted at them, wincing at the pain. "Do it!" They looked at me and didn't budge. My ties with them were just as deep as his.

Deeper. We were all the same age, kids who grew up on the corner together. Frankie was the older one, a dude who used to push us around when we were little, someone who still pushed too much.

"Yo, homes, you need to get to the hospital," Junie said to Frankie. "Your arm is lookin' bad."

"C'mon, let's get out of here," Chago said, reaching a hand down to Frankie.

"No. He's not going anywhere," I said then. "You all can go, but me and Frankie got something to finish."

Frankie turned to me, hatred in his

eyes. I could see he was struggling with the pain. His arm was starting to turn blue.

"You feelin' brave with that bat in your hand, homes? Think you're gonna finish me off just like that?" he hissed, spitting at me. "I always thought you'd be the one to challenge me. But you're too soft. You don't have it in you."

Part of me wanted to finish it right there, the way it might happen on the street. A heavy swing of the bat, and I could end it all. His life. Mine.

Maybe you'd read it in the papers or hear it on the news. Another gang-related murder, the reporters would say, making me seem like a monster.

"Don't do this, Martin. C'mon, homes, just let him go," Chago said.

"Why, so he can come back and finish what he came here to do?" I said.

Chago shook his head. He didn't understand the lesson Huero's death, César's injury, and Mr. Mitchell's story taught me. That I had to break from the street before it broke me.

"Whatcha waitin' for, homes? I ain't got all day," Frankie challenged, his useless, broken arm swelling by the minute.

"The police," I said, hearing the first

siren in the distance. "I was going to call them, but in this neighborhood your gunshot took care of that for me."

Chago's eyes opened wide. Junie looked at me like I'd just spoken a strange language.

"I told you he ratted us out. He's a snitch. You're dead, Martin. *Dead!*" Frankie said, spit falling from his mouth.

"No, I'm more alive than you'll ever know," I yelled back at him, smashing the bat into the doorframe near his shoulder. The crew took a step back like I had a disease they could catch.

"I never ratted on any of you. Not after you crippled that kid at the party last year. Not after I found out that kid was Hector's brother and that's why he was shooting at us. Not after I figured out your stupid temper cost my brother his life and put another guy in a wheelchair. Not even after you put me in the hospital. No, Frankie, I never ratted you out. But I'm gonna do it now. You're going down, homes, and Hector's going with you. Huero's gonna have justice."

Something new flickered in Frankie's eyes then. It flashed for a second, and I'll never forget it. Fear. He glanced over at

Junie and Jesus, then at Chago. "C'mon, homes. Let's get outta here. I ain't waitin' here for no cops." He moved toward the hallway when I raised the bat again, blocking his path.

"You ain't goin' nowhere, Frankie," I warned. "This is it. You're stayin' here with me."

Chago backed away from him, looked at Huero's picture and then at me, and nodded. Jesus and Junie shook their heads and started walking away.

"You took it too far, Frankie. You always did," Chago said. "Later, Martin."

"Later, homes," I said as they walked out.

Frankie cursed, and in one swift motion tried to shove past me. But I jabbed the bat into his right arm, and he went down in agony.

"I told you this ain't done," Frankie hissed as he heard the sirens approaching. "It ain't never gonna be done between you and me. Remember that."

"No, it's done this time, Frankie," I said, looking at Huero's picture. "It's finally done."

For months, it had been a maze, but it all made sense now. I would tell Officer Ramirez what I saw at last summer's party. That would point the police to César and show them why Hector was shooting at us. They'd finally have the case they'd need to bust him. I'd make sure of it.

Huero's killer would be off the streets. And Frankie would pay, too, for crippling a kid and for coming after me with a gun. He might also have to answer to Hector's crew for what he did.

No matter what, my mother and I finally had answers. We'd finally have peace.

Frankie didn't say anything when the police arrived, but I showed them the gun and the bullet hole in my floor. Told them I used the bat in self-defense. I told them the truth.

My mother and Officer Ramirez rushed in as the police took Frankie away. For hours, I told them what happened, made sure Ramirez heard every detail. Watched him write it all down.

Maybe you'd have handled it differently, I don't know. But for me, there was no other way. If I didn't act, there'd probably be more dead kids right now. And I would have been one of them. I may still be one day. But not *this* day.

"Thank God I didn't lose you

tonight," my mother said over and over again after the police left.

"No, Ma. You didn't lose me," I said, feeling my eyes burn as the sun began to rise.

The wounds from Huero's death will never fully heal. The past will always haunt me. But there is a future too, a life I need to live—for Huero and for me. It's something I can't just toss away, not after all I've seen, felt, and lost.

"I'm still here," I said to her, feeling something new stir in my chest. A glimmer of hope.

"Thanks to Huero, I'm still here."

Mr. Gates grunts at the last words of my story, still hanging in the air like a prayer.

"Thanks to Huero, I'm still here."

He clears his throat. Overhead, the lights of the auditorium are beaming down. The room is crowded but suddenly very quiet. Even the rows of students, parents, and teachers are silent.

"Mr. Luna," Mr. Gates begins finally. "I want to thank you for having the courage to explain your situation to us tonight. I appreciate your honesty. This is a difficult decision. Does anyone have anything else to add on this matter?"

I hear people begin to mumble. Mr. Gates raises his eyebrows in surprise.

"Yes, sir. We do," says a familiar voice.

I turn back to see Mr. Mitchell. He's standing with Vicky, Eric, and a small group of other students. Some are wearing Bluford football jerseys, teammates of Steve's that I barely knew. I don't understand what's happening.

"Mr. Gates," Mr. Mitchell says. "I join a number of my students in support of Martin Luna. We know this incident was not provoked by Martin. While he may not have handled it well, we feel—"

"That won't be necessary, Mr. Mitchell, but I applaud you and your students for coming forward," Mr. Gates says, closing his folder.

I brace myself for the words that are about to crash down on me like boulders.

"In my time at this school, I have heard many stories from kids like yourself who are struggling in our school. It seems each year the obstacles our young people face get worse," he says, shaking his head.

"Now, Martin, I can see you are a sensitive and thoughtful young man.

And I am sorry for your loss and the troubles you've had to endure these months. However, I cannot tolerate the behavior you have shown since you've arrived at this school," he pauses.

The auditorium is silent for a second. I know his next words will knock me out of Bluford for good. I can barely breathe.

"*But*, given the details you've provided and what I've witnessed at this meeting tonight, I don't think expulsion is necessary at this point. You can remain here at Bluford High School, provided you meet weekly with the school psychologist, Dr. Boyd. However, if there is another incident this year, I will reverse my decision. Understand, Martin?" He's staring right at me, his blue eyes sharp and focused.

I feel dizzy. Is it true what he just said? Is he serious?

"Yes, sir," I blurt out. "Thank you, sir. Thank you."

The group behind me begins to clap, and I feel my mother embrace me, sobbing with joy. Over her shoulder, I see the people who came to the hearing and stood up for me. Snitches like Eric and Vicky, the bravest people I know.

"Thank you," I mouth the words to

them, to Mr. Mitchell, and then to the sky for Huero. I know he's up there somewhere watching, smiling down at me this very moment.

Mr. Mitchell was right when he said life is about making choices. I finally made mine.

I'm not perfect. I lose it sometimes, and I still have enemies at Bluford. But Huero gave me a second chance. For him, my mother, and me, I am going to take that chance and reach for the sky with it. That's my choice.

I tell Huero this as I look for him in the bright lights overhead.

"Oh my God, Martin. You did it," Vicky says as she runs over to me. I feel her hugging me as I squint up at the lights. "*You did it!*"

Tears start rolling down my face, and I let them fall away.

Have you read the other books in the Bluford Series?

Search for Safety

John Langan

BLUFORD SERIES TP

(continued on the following pages)

The Bluford Series

Lost and Found	Blood Is Thicker
A Matter of Trust	Brothers in Arms
Secrets in the Shadows	Summer of Secrets
Someone to Love Me	The Fallen
The Bully	Shattered
The Gun	Search for Safety
Until We Meet Again	

The Townsend Library

The Adventures of Huckleberry Finn
The Adventures of Tom Sawyer
The Beasts of Tarzan
Black Beauty
The Call of the Wild
Dracula
Ethan Frome
Everyday Heroes
Facing Addiction: Three True Stories
Frankenstein and Dr. Jekyll & Mr. Hyde
The Gods of Mars
Great Expectations
Great Stories of Suspense & Adventure
Gulliver's Travels
Incidents in the Life of a Slave Girl
It Couldn't Happen to Me: Three True Stories of Teenage Moms
Jane Eyre
The Jungle Book
The Last of the Mohicans
Laughter and Chills: Seven Great Stories
Letters My Mother Never Read
The Merry Adventures of Robin Hood
Narrative of the Life of Frederick Douglass
The Odyssey
The Prince and the Pauper
The Princess of Mars
Reading Changed My Life! Three True Stories
The Red Badge of Courage
The Return of the Native
The Return of Tarzan
Silas Marner
Sister Carrie
The Story of Blima: A Holocaust Survivor
Surviving Abuse: Four True Stories
Swiss Family Robinson
A Tale of Two Cities
Tarzan of the Apes
Ten Real-Life Stories
Treasure Island
Uncle Tom's Cabin
Up from Slavery: An Autobiography
The Warlord of Mars
White Fang
The Wind in the Willows
The Wizard of Oz

**For more information,
visit www.townsendpress.com**